Take Me

ELLA JACOBS

ENSLAVED SERIES
BOOK ONE

TAKE ME

Copyright © 2024 by Ella Jacobs

http://www.ellajacobs.com

ISBN 978-87-975517-0-7

First Edition: October 2024

SHA-256 hash: eff8c6be56491aeb046e5218c
22a6ffdf56fe74f7432cefd2d3c399022fea41b

*To all the girls who want their knight in
shining armor cloaked in black morals.
There's no romantic rescue here.*

TO MY DOM

On a sunny day at a harbor in Southern Spain, my Dom painted a vivid picture for me: A cold basement, the echoing clicks of approaching steps, and a woman waiting fearfully in a cell.

I wrote most of this dark and desolate story to the backdrop of a blue sky, palm trees, and sunshine glittering on the water, while the man who feeds my light and darkness whispered depravities into my ear.

I finished the story in the same place a year later, with the same man at my side.

Thank you, S, for being my inspiration, my rock, and the man who fulfills all my dirty desires.

Warning:
No Hearts and Roses Ahead

Dear reader

The trigger list for this book is **long and heavy**.

If you have any triggers at all, check out the list on ellajacobs.com before proceeding.

If you do however want to be shocked and disturbed, go ahead and join me on this smutty, dark journey where manipulation and conditioning thrive and no forced orgasm is too many.

Please read responsibly.

Lots of dark love
Ella

CHAPTER

1

"Have you ever been choked?" Nikolai asks, sliding his hand onto my neck with a featherlight touch that sends a flurry of shivers down my arm.

"No," I gasp as he positions his fingers on my pulse points.

"Do you know what happens if I press here?"

I shake my head as I pant through parted lips, my pulse pounding against his fingers.

"I can take your breath away in two ways. If I press here, I'll shut off the oxygen to your brain." He snaps his fingers. "In a matter of seconds, you're out." He moves across my skin until his palm rests in a snug fit around my throat. "But if I press here." He gives a slight squeeze that tightens at the front of my neck. "I'll shut off the air that goes into your lungs."

He tightens further, and his breaths grow heavy as he revels in the power of controlling something as crucial as my ability to breathe. The pressure in my head builds as the blood gathers there, but what is far more frightening is the constriction on my windpipe. I can still breathe almost normally, but the threat is stark and obtrusive.

"It will take a lot longer before you pass out this way." Caressing my arm with his knuckles, he speaks in a gentle tone. "I'll get to enjoy your struggle as your strength slowly drains from your body."

Fear becomes a speedy swoosh in my veins.

I shouldn't let him do this. I really shouldn't.

Five days of hot sex is no way near enough to let a man twice my size put me in such a vulnerable position. Especially not one I've just met at some Romanian bar and don't know anything about—except that he's Russian and loaded, which is a major red flag in itself. But I also shouldn't have let him tie me down or spank me after four days. But that ship has already sailed.

"Do you trust me?" he asks in his delicious, accented baritone, leaning so close that his hot breath tickles my ear.

His strength is carefully controlled as he presses a little harder, restricting my breath to small gulps of air. And maybe this is why I nod. It's a minuscule motion against his massive hand, but I mean it. I trust him not to harm me. That measured control feels safe.

"Hmm," he rumbles, satisfied with my response. "Then maybe I should take it a step further."

A tiny mewl is my only response before he clamps his other hand over my mouth and pinches my nose between two fingers.

Terror crawls across my skin even as heat spreads through my core.

I inhale hard against his hand, hoping for a crack

between his fingers—a tiny opening at the edge. But no such luck. His hand is massive, the seal tight.

I writhe against him to test how helpless I am, and the result is the same. My strength is no match for his. I might be fairly strong for my petite size, but it's like comparing a rabbit to a lion. He's over six feet tall with a natural broad build and well-defined muscles.

So I accept defeat and sink into him, seeking his strength to balance out the feeling of being a tiny flower in a field full of trampling feet.

"You don't have any control." His voice takes on a dark edge that makes me doubt if I really did read him right—if his control isn't more dangerous than safe. "If I want to end you right here and now, I'll just hold on a little longer. There's nothing you can do about it. Not even with your hands free."

Doubt swirls in my mind as the need to breathe convulses in my lungs. I groan against his hand in an effort to let him know I've had enough. He has read me well enough during the last few days of kinky exploration, always pausing when he hits a limit, so he will this time too.

I hope.

"Go ahead," he coaxes. "See if I'm right."

"Mm, mm," I whimper, trying to shake my head. This is not fun anymore. I really need to breathe.

He releases my throat to stroke my hair. The gesture is gentle and loving, but the hand over my mouth remains. The loss of his grip on my neck should give me a chance to break free, but when I jerk against him, there's no give.

Panic builds in my oxygen-starved system, and I put in all my strength as I struggle against his strong body and shoot my hands up to yank at his arm.

But it's still no use. With one single hand, he has me in a vise, and the other hand seems to mock me with the fact as he keeps caressing. Blurry spots form in my vision, and the strength seeps from my limbs, rendering me even more helpless.

All I can think is that I shouldn't be here. Stupid, stupid me. I fell for a charming businessman, went with him to his hotel, and let him introduce me to a world of kink I'd always dreamed of exploring but never dared to. I put my trust in him because he seemed convincing and in control of his dark urges.

And now I'm going to pay the ultimate price.

Tears trickle down my cheeks as the realization settles into my mind. But my pussy is happy and wet, having had the time of its life. If it could voice an opinion, it would say it was all worth it.

But it's not. Nothing is worth dying in the arms of a psychopath.

I jerk as the last energy drains from my body and darkness slithers along the edges of my mind. The only life left within me is the stuttering in my lungs as they are still trying to access precious oxygen.

"Hmm," he hums as he wraps an arm around my waist to steady my weight. "I love seeing you on the brink of consciousness. And I'd love to see you lose it too." He presses a sweet kiss to the top of my head, and I twitch in one last feeble attempt at escape as the darkness closes in. But just before it can claim me, he releases my mouth. "But I want to hear your screams again."

The oxygen is an assault on my lungs as I suck in a huge gulp of air. It stings my deprived tissues and sets my blood swooshing through my veins to carry new vitality through my system.

The shock wrenches a sob from my throat, and suddenly, I'm shaking all over, heaving to access air for a whole different reason. I hug my arms around myself in a poor attempt to soothe the shaken feeling rattling in my body.

Nikolai turns me around in his arms and cradles me against him, offering the comfort I badly need. But I don't want him. He's the one who caused this distress.

"No. Let me go." I try to pull away, but he won't let me.

"Shh," he simply soothes, curving a gentle hand around the back of my head.

"Let me go!" I cry over and over. My words blend with uncontrollable sobs as I bang my fists against his chest. "I hate you, you sick bastard. I fucking hate you!"

Moving two fingers between my legs, he slides into my wetness and thrusts straight into my pussy. "I don't think you do."

"Ah!" I cry, bucking against him.

He pumps in and out with punishing force, and I'm mortified to hear the slick sound coming from between my thighs. I'm even more horrified to hear the moans blending into the mix of sounds coming up my throat.

But my brain has no capacity to linger on the wrongness of it all. The pain and the desire crashing inside me take up all room and render rational thought impossible.

"Noo," I protest, yet I cling to his thick arms and burrow my head against his naked chest as I keep crying and moaning. Because he's the only source of comfort—the only stability I can find in this chaos. And the only one who can deliver me from this raging need that suddenly has my entire body teetering on the edge.

Grabbing me by the arms, he throws me onto the bed. He slides down beside me, wrapping me up in his arms as he sinks his massive length into me. "I've got you," he reassures, stroking my hair out of my face and pressing kisses to my tear-stained cheeks as he fucks me. "Let go and let me take control over you, just like I did your breath. I won't let anything happen to you."

God, his words melt away my last resistance. They're full of the same promise that made me fall for him in the first place. The promise of safety amidst the storm.

So I release what little control I have left and come apart in his arms. I shudder through the rolling currents of my orgasm, curling my toes and arching my back even as the tears keep falling.

"Good girl," he whispers against my hair. His fingers dig into my hips as he jerks against me, his movements stuttering as he finds his own release. "Such. A good. Fucking. Girl."

* * *

"Are you okay?" Nikolai asks, tucking his white shirt into his pants, when I come out of the bathroom.

I stop in the middle of the enormous hotel suite and wrap the towel tighter around myself. "I think so," I say tentatively. Nikolai spent an hour holding me after he fucked me, but remnants of the panicked fear he instilled within me still linger, making me feel frazzled and fragile.

"Come here." He sits on the bed and pats the spot beside him.

I tiptoe across the space and gingerly sink onto the white sheets.

Wrapping an arm around my shoulders, he presses his lips to my hair. "I'm sorry I scared you, but I'm also not sorry. I needed to test your boundaries before we part ways. I've been with too many women who say they're into kinky shit, pleasure and pain and all that, only to run away screaming when I step beyond playful sadism. I couldn't wait a month or two to find out. Not with my busy schedule."

Part of me gets him. Once this week is over, it will be a while before we can see each other again. I'm going hiking in the Carpathian Mountains for two weeks, and when I get back, he will have left the country and will have a full month of back-to-back meetings and various business engagements to attend to in different parts of the world. So who knows when we'll get to see each other again? I've considered cutting another week off my hiking trip—maybe skipping it altogether—to get more time with him, but when I told him that idea last night, he immediately shot it down, promising he'd make sure we'd see each other again soon.

"You couldn't have waited two more days at least?" I chance a glance up at him and meet a grave expression.

"I couldn't. I need time with you after such brutality—to make sure you're okay and to handle any drops."

"I'm okay," I say.

Nikolai grabs my chin, forcing me to stare into the blazing intensity of his gaze. "You're not."

I flit my eyes up and down, suddenly feeling uncertain. And scared. Is he going to cast me aside now because I didn't pass the test and can't handle his dark brand of dominance?

Sure, it was more than intense. It was terrifying, really. But God, the thrill. The thought of never getting to experience such a high again—to be without his expert touch—makes it hard to breathe.

"I'm sorry I couldn't live up to your expectations." I push off the bed and hurry toward my pile of clothes in the fancy armchair. I knew this man was way out of my league from the start. I knew it would end with me getting hurt.

He's behind me in an instant, tossing away the jeans I was holding and snatching me by the back of my neck.

The air leaves me with a thud as he shoves me up against the wall, and God help me, I can't stop myself from arching back into him. I'm so goddamn helpless with this man in every sense of the word; I can't even control my body.

And he's too observant to let any small reaction slip past him.

Locking his free hand onto my hip, he holds me in the alluring position and presses the hard bulge in his pants against my ass.

"I'm not done with you," he sneers into my ear. "The things I'm gonna do to you..." he trails off, leaving the dark promise hanging.

"I thought I couldn't handle you," I retort with reckless irritation.

He lets out a low chuckle—a sinister one that has icy chills skating down my skin, shuddering in my bones. "You can't. But you're the first woman who's even gotten close, so now you have to."

He tightens his grip around my neck with a strength that makes me yelp. Again, I think how reckless I am. I should have left when I had the chance. Before he takes it a step further. And one more. Until he decides he wants to snuff out my breath for good.

I've seen the darkness in his eyes. At first, I thought it was a mere reflection of the primal nature of his sexual energy, but now I think it runs much deeper.

Still, I can't keep from moaning when he shoves a finger between my legs, flicking it over my clit and stirring crazy arousal within seconds.

"You're mine now," he whispers into my ear. "You'd better get used to that idea. Because there's no backing out."

His words light up the alarm bells in my head anew. I flatten my hands on the wall and try to push back, maybe flee this hotel room altogether and never look back. But once again, he has me trapped with a single hand. So I try something else.

"I'm scared," I confess, feeling utterly vulnerable as the words leave my mouth.

Leaning close, he brushes his fingers along my

cheek, his voice softening to accompany the gentleness. "I know. It's so fucking beautiful. The way you tremble beneath my touch even as you arch for more." He releases my neck to slide both arms around me, pressing me into his warm body as he whispers. "You're perfect."

No man has ever scared me so much, and no man has ever made me feel so safe. The combination is like a drug, clouding my mind and sending a thrilling rush through my veins.

I lean back into him, throwing all good judgment out the window as I bare myself to him. "I'm scared you're going to hurt me."

He turns me around and leans down to press his lips to mine in an intimate kiss that has our tongues dancing together in perfect harmony. It all comes naturally. I've never had such an effortless, wonderful kiss.

"I am going to hurt you," he says bluntly as he breaks the kiss and slips his hand into my auburn hair, grabbing it close to the roots as if to prove his point. "But I'm always gonna put you back together like I did after I took your breath. Can you trust that?"

"I don't know." I search his eyes for some kind of reassurance. And I do find it. But I also find as many reasons not to trust him. "I want to, but..."

He relieves me of the burden of explaining. "Don't worry. It'll come. For now, just let me prove it to you again." He presses down on my shoulders. "Get on your knees and take out my cock."

I land on the floor with a thud and scramble to open his belt and zipper. His cock springs free, long and hard.

"Take it in your mouth," he demands, wrapping my

long hair around his hand in a firm grip that has pins and needles prickling at the back of my head.

I grab the base and dart my tongue across the tip.

"In your mouth," he scolds, and before I can obey, he pulls my head forward, filling my mouth with his massive size and hitting the back of my throat.

My stomach contracts, and I cough and sputter around him as I try to subdue the urge to gag.

He tuts. "No one's taught you how to take a cock in your throat?"

I shake my head around the thick intrusion.

"Then we'll have to do it the hard way. I don't have the time to teach you." He draws back enough to tip my head up. "Too bad for you." He swipes his thumb across my chin to catch a drop of spit. Then he digs both hands into my hair and holds me in place as he shoves forward. He keeps advancing, all the way to the back of my throat, even as I gag and gasp around him. "More fun for me," he adds with a satisfied grunt.

I clutch his thighs as spit drips from my mouth and water trickles from my eyes.

Scoffing, he says, "You are aware it's only halfway in, right? Before we're done here, your lips will be around the base. And I'll be deep inside your throat."

Panic flares in my mind at the thought. Shoving at his thighs, I moan and groan my protest, unable to form any sensical words around his length. But just like before, I'm helpless. I'm stuck here, at the mercy of this powerful stranger—stuck between my fear and lust.

"Oh yes, you're taking all of me. Relax your throat," he urges, reaching down to caress the front of my neck.

I let out a garbled sound in protest as I dig my nails into his thighs.

"I don't mind if you vomit around my cock, but I'm not so sure you'd like it, so I suggest you do as I say." He keeps stroking up and down, coaxing me to relax, even as he holds my hair with burning strength.

His unwavering power works its way into me, tugging at some strange place I never knew existed. He makes it sound so easy. Just obey and let him take care of the rest. It's so simple.

So I give in to his capable hands, relax my throat, and notice how the urge to gag eases.

"That's it," he praises on a long, languid breath. "Keep it like that. Steady breaths." He moves his hips, ever so slowly, pressing his cock forward. "Take a deep breath."

He pauses, and the air stutters past my lips as I inhale. There's just enough room around his cock to let it slip past, into my lungs, and when he moves another increment, the hole is fully blocked. I try to breathe again, but no air comes in, no air goes out.

Digging my hands into his thighs anew, I feel myself hovering on the precipice, about to crash into a new burst of panic.

Reading my reaction with startling precision, like he's done every other time he's pushed me, he says, "Don't worry, you have enough air to last a little longer. Just focus on relaxing your throat."

I close my eyes and direct my focus toward my neck. My muscles are tense again, and I imagine a warm flow of energy seeping through them and washing away the strain. It takes a couple of moments, but I manage, and pride swells inside me at his appraisal.

"Good girl. Keep going like that. Just forget about your breath. I'll let you have more air when needed. No asphyxiation this time. I promise."

His words send a current of heat coursing through me, making it easier to keep my muscles relaxed as he pushes a little farther. He repeats a few times, pushing on, then giving me a moment to adjust before advancing again. I'm so focused on taking his length that I barely notice the need for air twitch in my lungs. When he pulls out, I automatically drag in a large gulp.

Relief courses through me as I realize he kept his promise, and I crane my neck to look up at him with a smile tugging at my lips.

"You're doing so well." He slides his thumb across the edge of my mouth to catch a drop of spit. "But you still have a little ways to go."

He prods the thick head against my lips, and I eagerly open up, welcoming the salty taste of his precum. I've never cared much for blowjobs, but having Nikolai's cock in my mouth is as rewarding as it's scary—and the latter only drives the heated lust that seems to have become a constant hum since I met him.

As if reading my thoughts, he says, "Touch your fingers between your legs to see if my cunt is wet."

I make a garbled sound as he hits the back of my mouth, and I go still for a second as I work to subdue my gag reflex. Once I have it under control, I slip my fingers between my folds and go rigid once more as I feel the dripping slickness. I knew I was kinky, but I could have never imagined this much.

"Show me," Nikolai orders.

Blood seeps into my face, and I shake my head around his cock.

"Show me!" With a hand on the back of my head, he shoves himself into my throat, making me jerk and stutter from the suddenness. My stomach convulses as my gag reflex threatens to activate. I shoot my hand up, hoping it will make him pull out.

Nikolai grabs my wrist tight and draws back a smidgen, just enough to allow me a crack of air, and I'm so focused on breathing slowly and relaxing my muscles that I barely hear him tut. It's only when he speaks that I notice the mockery.

"You really are a horny little girl. Already slick and ready to take my cock again. It's a shame I want to use your mouth." He pulls out and locks his fingers around my jaw as he leans down to taunt me right in my face. "Such a horny little bitch like you shouldn't go wanting. I'll make sure you'll get all the cock your filthy pussy desires."

With a suddenness that has me reeling, he straightens and shoves straight back into my mouth. One long steady thrust until he's halfway down my throat.

"I can't wait to see what a good little sex toy you'll become."

I can't think, I can't move, I can't see. His violent dominance has wiped out everything except the need to obey, and his words barely even register as I put all my focus into taking his length as he works his way inside.

It takes a couple of tries and several pauses for air,

but finally, I'm able to take his full length. He sinks in place, rooted to the hilt, deep in my throat. My mind is mush, and I've lost control over my body. My hips keep grinding in hungry circles as my pussy drips onto the floor, drool spills in strings from my mouth, and my head lulls in Nikolai's commanding grip.

"You'll become such a good little whore, taking whatever cock I give you. Both mine and whatever men I whore you out to. You'll be such a horny little slut that you won't be able to think about anything else." Nikolai strokes his knuckles along my cheek, and I aim my blurry eyes up at him to find his expression firm with a dark promise that looks terrifyingly sincere. But I know the words are only meant to degrade and drive my lust, so I just moan my agreement, barely knowing what he's saying anyway.

It's only when he pulls out and starts masturbating in front of my face that some of the fog clears up. Surprised, I blink up at him and down at his moving hand. I thought he'd come in my mouth, but he clearly has other intentions, and his cock isn't even aimed at my head, but at the floor.

"Spread your legs," he demands.

I obey, and disappointment bears down on me as I realize he's going to come on the floor between my legs. It seems almost cruel after everything he just put me through, preparing my throat to take him. It's like I'm not worthy of him, and emotions well up inside me as I stare from my parted legs to his pumping hand and up at his emotionless face.

Nikolai tightens his grip on my hair when I try to

look away from his cock. "Watch it!"

I press my lips together as I try to rein in an acute sense of defeat, but a tear slips from my eyes anyway. It only seems to drive his lust. He lets out a groan and picks up speed, and his grip on my hair becomes so hard that I yelp as he shoots his cum onto the floor. Right between my legs. A cruel statement.

"Did you really think you deserved to taste my orgasm?" He yanks my hair back, forcing me to face his cruel expression. It's like seeing an entirely different man than the one who held me tenderly only a little while ago. I feel dirty and wrong, sitting here at the foot of a stranger and letting him degrade me like this. I have no idea what I'm doing.

I'm about to break into tears, but Nikolai breaks me from the hurt with a sharp command. "Lick it up."

My eyes go wide. "Wh—what?"

He sinks to his haunches in front of me, still holding my hair, and speaks in a frighteningly low tone that weighs the words down with his Russian accent. "I said. Lick. It. Up."

He shoves my head into the pool of cum, and I dart my tongue out to lap it up. Somewhere at the back of my mind, I feel warped and depraved, but his command has blotted out what little ability to think was left in my mind. So I keep licking like a mindless beast as he smears my head around in the pool of our juices.

"Such a good little bitch." His words are as full of taunt as praise, and the combination drives me deeper into the base state where I'm nothing but his to use. It's as harrowing as it's freeing, and I keep whimpering and

16

sniffling even as my body thrums with desire.

When he finally lets me sit up on my knees again, I just stare at him, unable to care about the sticky mess on my face and my runny nose.

"Such a dirty little girl." He tuts and swipes a thumb through the mess on my face. "Come here, my sweet *Lisichka*," he says, calling me the Russian diminutive for fox as he pulls me into his arms, and I mold my body into his like I was made to be there. A peace unlike anything I've ever felt settles over me as he strokes my hair and holds me like I'm the most precious thing in the world.

* * *

Two days later, Nikolai has his driver take us to the train station to send me off to the Carpathian Mountains and let me enjoy the vacation I had planned.

The sun is setting beyond the tracks as we walk hand in hand toward the far end of the platform to get a little privacy while we wait for my train.

A twisty, wistful sort of feeling tightens my stomach and mixes with the butterflies that have been flapping constantly for a week. I clasp Nikolai's big hand in an effort to alleviate the queasiness.

"You're awfully quiet." He sets my backpack and a plastic bag with some mysterious contents on the concrete ground and presses a reassuring hand to my arm. "I don't think I've seen you this quiet since I met you." He makes this amused lift of his eyebrows. "Not even when I was inside you."

My cheeks heat. I'm a bit of a screamer. At least with Nikolai. My throat is still raw from all the staggering orgasms he's given me.

I give him a careful smile. "I was quiet when you took my breath."

His amusement fades and gives way to something dark and threatening. Lifting his fingers to my neck, he grazes the hollow at my windpipe and watches my throat bob as I gulp. "*That* made you very quiet."

I tip my head back a little, baring the vulnerable spot to this stranger. I know it's reckless, but I trust him. If he wanted to harm me, he had plenty of chances.

"I'll do that again." He moves his eyes back to mine, leveling me with a serious expression. "But there are a few things you need to learn first."

"Like what?"

His nostrils flare with something feral that sends a surge of fear through me. It's the same sensation I've felt over and over again through the last week, but instead of letting it fester in my chest, I let it roll on to gather in heated throbs between my legs.

"You'll see. All in good time."

I sigh. I don't want to see 'in good time.' I want it all right now.

"Come here." With an arm around my waist, he pulls me into him and wraps me in a tight hug.

This time, my sigh is peaceful. As quickly as he can set my pulse pounding with fear, he can make it settle into a tranquil rhythm. I fold my arms between us and soak up the feeling of his strong, wide chest and inhale his rich, earthy scent that makes me think of pine trees and wet moss. One of my favorite scents in the world.

He holds me close, creating a safe nest for me in his warm embrace. Curling up against him, becoming all small and vulnerable, has been the most natural thing in the world since the first time he took me in his arms. It's part of the dynamic that has crackled between us from the first moment our eyes locked at the bar where we met. He's the masculine pole to my femininity. He takes control and I give it up.

I can't believe it's only been a week. He might still be a stranger in most ways, but he feels familiar and safe as I press myself into him—like I've known him for months. It's crazy how quickly I've grown attached to this man. Scary, really. But it also feels right. Like he's strong enough to carry the responsibility of the uncertainty—strong enough to carry my burdens.

And maybe most of all, it's easy to trust him because I know I'm not the only one who senses that something big is happening here. He feels it too. He said it himself, and so does his every touch, kiss, and heated look.

He wants me as much as I want him.

And maybe that's why I'm bold enough to say the words, "I don't want to go hiking."

"Shh." He draws back to curve a hand around my cheek, and I lean into his touch as I fall captive to his attentive gaze. "You'll see me again soon. I promise."

He says it with a startling sincerity that makes me want to go even less. Usually, I'm not overly outspoken, but this man does things to me no one before has—including throwing my propriety out the window.

"Can't I come with you?" I blurt, only feeling a

twinge of embarrassment at my bluntness.

He moves his thumb back and forth over my cheekbone. "No."

God, his rejection hurts a little. Biting my lip, I look away, then back at him. "When will I see you again?"

His lips tip up in a gentle smile as his eyes warm with affection. "Before you know it."

I can't help my disappointed tone. "Okay." I'd really like a specific answer. I don't do well with these kinds of uncertainties. Especially not with something this important.

"I look forward to it." He leans down to press his lips to my forehead, then takes the plastic bag he brought and retrieves something red and fluffy that he hands to me. "This is for you—to remember me when you feel lonely."

A huge smile spreads across my face as I take the red fox teddy and look into the cutest golden-rimmed eyes. I take one of the fluffy ears between my fingers and swipe the inside as I remember how he touched the little fox pendant on my bracelet the first night we met.

It had only been five minutes since he slipped onto the bar stool beside me when he reached for the silver fox. "Is this your favorite animal?" he asked, and I clearly recall the flurry of shivers shuddering up my arm as his fingers brushed my skin. The whole world dissipated as he twirled a lock of my hair and said, "A pretty little *Lisichka*."

He told me it's the Russian diminutive for fox, and he's been calling me that ever since.

Licking my lips, I snap out of the memory.

"You remembered?" I say, gazing up at him with

wide, vulnerable eyes.

Hands folded behind his back, he watches me like he can read every flicker of emotion in my features. "Of course I did."

I search his face, thinking I see something hidden in there. Something that goes beyond normal affection—a possessive hunger that shouldn't be possible after only seven days.

But his face remains impassive, and I have not known him long enough to tell if this is a normal or extraordinary expression for him.

Maybe I'm just hoping.

But when the train rolls in and he leans down to press his lips to mine, the kiss holds the same intensity I thought I saw somewhere deep in the stoic lines of his face. And not just the kiss. His entire body.

Seizing my lower arms, he shoves them onto my back, forcing me into strict compliance as he angles his head to deepen the kiss.

"Mine," he whispers, his hands tightening with the force of his words.

I pant as I stare up at him, and my feet shuffle on the concrete as my balance wavers.

But I don't need my balance. I'm trapped in Nikolai's grip, and he keeps me steady.

So I sag against him, my hips lifting to his as I lean into his grip.

"Your body already knows." He lifts his chin, his nostrils flaring with primal dominance. "Soon, your mind will too."

I can't speak; I can't think. At this very moment, I

truly am his. Mind and body. I want to stay like this forever—trapped by his eyes, his hands, his unrelenting will. Consumed so fully that I forget about myself. But all too soon, he leans down for a final kiss and releases me.

"See you soon, my sweet *Lisichka*."

The world staggers beneath me, and I stare straight ahead with unfocused eyes as he picks up my bag and holds a strap out for me. When I lift my arm, I realize I'm still holding onto the teddy. I shift it from hand to hand as I push my arms through the straps, then hug it tight against my chest as I approach the train with precarious steps.

Grabbing the handrail, I set my foot on the first step and turn to look back.

Nikolai gives me a firm nod that seems to say everything I need to hear—the gentle promise to see me again, the dark anticipation of all the things he'll do to me, and the possessiveness that thrills me as much as it scares me.

It takes me a while to recover from the heady effect of Nikolai as I settle in the train seat.

I'm slow and confused when the conductor comes to see my ticket, and he gives me a stern look as I fumble through several pockets in my bag before finding the little piece of paper.

"Can I see some ID?" the chubby man with a mustache and thick accent says.

"ID?" I frown at him. Well, that's a new one. But I fish out my driver's license anyway and hand it to him.

"Julie Thomsen?" he says like it's a question.

"That's me."

Without further comment or question, he hands it back to me. And then he's gone again.

Strange man.

I lean my head back against the seat and turn my attention to the setting sun outside the windows. The city is already thinning out, giving way to large, open fields. Soon, it will be mountains and trees. The peaceful quiet of untouched nature.

It will do me good to get out there. A couple of weeks to clear my mind and let the butterflies settle. Even impatient as I am, I don't want to rush into anything. This will give me time to see things from a different perspective—look for any red flags my smitten eyes are unable to see.

No need to hurry. Nikolai will still be there when I get back. I open my eyes and look down at the teddy. *There's no doubt that he will.*

CHAPTER

2

I'm about to drift off when a hand taps my shoulder. Blinking the sleepiness from my eyes, I look up to see the chubby conductor with a wide mustache.

"You've already seen my ticket."

"I'm gonna have to ask you to move to the last car," he says in an accent so thick I'm not sure I heard it right.

"I'm sorry?"

"The last car," he repeats in a not-so-friendly tone, taking off his hat and swiping at his sweaty hair.

"Why?" I glance around at the many empty seats. It's not like there's not enough room here, so I can't think of any good reason as to why he needs me to move.

He takes my backpack from the seat beside me, slings it over his shoulder, and gestures for me to go ahead.

Too tired to argue, I slide out from the seat and step into the aisle. Another irritated hand gesture has me moving toward the end of the car. I almost feel like a thief being escorted from a building as the conductor follows close behind.

The last car is completely empty, and I ignore an eerie sensation as I settle in one of the seats a little way down the hall. The conductor places my bag in the seat beside me and walks away without another word.

Once he's gone, I take out my phone to check Facebook. It's my favorite way to stay in touch with friends back home whenever I go on one of my hiking trips.

A little red dot informs me I have ten notifications, and I frown as I click on it and find one of my friends having commented on a post: *Why Italy?*

Why Italy, indeed? I have no idea what she means, so I open the post and stare incredulously at the screen as I see an update I haven't written. But it's my name, my picture.

Change of plans. I've set my sights on the Dolomites. Online access will be patchy, so I might be offline for a while.

My heart pounds in my rib cage. Has someone hacked my account?

I press the reply button and type out a message, explaining that my plans remain the same and I've been hacked. But nothing happens when I hit send, so I copy the text and refresh the page, only to get a white screen.

Turning my eyes to the thick forest below a darkening sky, I curse under my breath. No service when I most need it, of course.

Fuck it. It doesn't matter that people think I'm headed for Italy for another hour. So I shut off my phone and close my eyes, trying to expel the scary questions pressing for attention in my mind.

* * *

The sound of screeching metal stirs me from a deep sleep, and I jolt in my seat as the train comes to a stop.

As I peel my eyes open, I find pitch-black darkness outside the windows. No lights from a station platform, no cars, no people. Only dead still darkness and the shadows of mountains looming in the distance.

Great! The train gives out in the middle of nowhere. You really can't trust things to run smoothly in this part of Europe. I've learned this firsthand more than once.

Hopefully, it's just a minor issue and we'll be up and running again in half an hour or so.

I close my eyes and lean my head back to let sleep take me back in its gentle arms.

But the peace is brief.

The sound of movement behind me jolts me wide awake. My eyes fly open, and a gust of air blows across my skin just before something descends over my head. A hood or a bag. Thick enough to cover my world in darkness. Then hands press down on my shoulders to keep the hood—or me—in place.

Terror pounds through my veins, and I burst into uncoordinated panic. Shooting my arms up, I rip at the hands. Rip at the fabric. Squirm in the seat and try to wriggle down, out of the bag.

But it's no use. The hands are like two vises, pinning me back against the seat with terrifying ease.

A shrill sound fills the air around me, and it takes me

a moment to realize it's my own scream. I can't stop it, and I can't stop my frantic struggle.

A hand releases my shoulder to snake around my throat, probing a bit before digging into the sides. My airflow remains intact, but the strength seems to drain from my very bones. Terror blazes in my mind as I remember what Nikolai said as he pressed against my pulse points. *In a matter of seconds, you're out.*

My scream dies, darkness descends over my mind, and I sag in the seat, hovering on the precipice of consciousness.

Before the darkness can claim me whole, the fingers relax, and awareness seeps back in. But it's slow and muddled, and it takes me a moment to remember what's going on.

Someone is beside me too—someone big. His enormous size is evident when his muscular shoulder brushes my arm and when a hefty, calloused hand grabs my wrist.

It's not the same one who shoved the bag over my head. That man is still behind my seat, holding my droopy head in the crook of his arm as he secures a knot on the bag.

There are two of them.

And the one in the aisle is tying knots at my hands. Ropes around my wrists.

The realizations filter in one at a time, filling my head with an urgency I can't act upon. At least not until it's too late.

Once my limbs wake up, the ropes are already secured, locking my hands firmly together. I make an effort, anyway, twisting my wrists against the coarse material. But there's no give.

"No, no, no, no," I whimper as I squirm, putting in more energy as my strength returns. I try to twist my head and bite the arm around my neck, but the man behind me simply traps my head against the seat with a hand on my forehead.

So I kick my legs instead when the bulky man grabs my foot. But my body either hasn't regained all its strength, or he's simply too strong. Within seconds, he has my feet gathered with rope and is securing the knot.

I make a final attempt at getting free, but the effort sends a stab of defeat through me as I become achingly aware of how trapped I am. Head, hands, feet. And with the way my head is stuck, I can only move my body a few inches.

Hopelessness sets in, devastating and severe. The knowledge that these two men are going to take me no matter what I do burns through my mind.

Choking terror infiltrates my system, twisting my gut and squeezing my chest so hard I can't breathe.

I feel like I'm drowning as I heave for air without getting any. All I achieve is getting fabric into my mouth and blocking my airway further.

Panic wraps my mind in dizzying colors, reducing me to frantic instincts. I claw at the fabric with my bound hands as I pant with shallow gasps.

"Breathe in through your nose," a deep, accented voice says close to my ear, pushing my bound hands back into my lap with surprising gentleness. "Out through your mouth."

Readjusting his hand on my forehead into an almost calm grip, he takes a loud breath through his nose as if to spur me on.

I try to imitate but only manage a superficial breath.

"One more," he urges, flattening his other hand over my chest. The weight should be oppressive, but it's not. It's something else. Soothing, I think.

My entire body shudders as I drag in a long breath through my nose, and another wave of shivers rolls through me as I push the air back out through my mouth. The fabric billows slightly over my head, but it doesn't stick to my mouth, and with a few more repetitions, I find that it's possible to breathe through it.

The man behind me releases me, and I'm a bit disturbed to find myself missing the warm hands.

The man at my side hoists me up, and a strangled gasp escapes me as I land over his shoulder with a thud. Now I can truly feel his size, and it's even more frightening than I thought at first. His shoulder is wide and solid like it's made for carrying a body, and his back is hard plains of solid muscle under my head.

It takes all my focus to breathe as I bounce in time to his long strides. He, on the other hand, doesn't seem to strain the least as he carries me through the car. I think I'm no more than a sack of potatoes to him.

Part of me wants to bang my fists against his back, but I already know the outcome, and my brief panic attack seems to have drained all my energy. So I just hang there, and when the chilly night air lets me know we're leaving the train, he easily passes me to his partner.

The new man—or rather, the one who put the sack

over my head—takes me in his arms, holding me close to his chest as he walks. He's not as bulky as the other man, but I feel the devastating strength in the effortless way he handles me, nonetheless. I wouldn't stand a chance even if it had only been him.

The realization is not enough to deter me from launching into another fit of struggles when I hear the train screeching against the tracks. The sound jolts me from my paralysis, and I start writhing and whimpering, not caring that I might fall from his arms and crash hard. I just need to get back on that train, no matter what it takes.

"Don't waste your energy," he simply says, but his words only ramp up my furious energy. And then I'm screaming again.

I expect him to act quickly, cover my mouth to muffle the sound or grab my throat again, but he just keeps on walking without a care in the world. It scares me shitless, and I'm headed straight for a new panic attack when he dumps me onto something hard—a surface, box, something half-enclosed.

A trunk, I realize as my fingers grapple and find a steely edge.

A large hand presses against my chest, and I can't figure out if it's meant to soothe or subdue.

It works both ways.

I go still beneath its weight, and when the man drags in a loud breath through his nose, I automatically follow.

He repeats a few times until I go still, breathing somewhat steadily.

"Seriously, don't waste your breath screaming." He's

close this time, the deep timbre of his voice resonating close to my ear. "No one but the bears will hear you, and I'll be quite disappointed to come back here and find my merchandise having choked on her own screams."

His words stun me into silence, and I don't move when he proceeds to tie a rope between my wrists and legs. Finally, he stuffs a few big pillows around me to create a sort of tight nest.

"No bruises except the ones we allow," he explains, shoving a final pillow into the space above my head. "Remember to breathe," he says, and then there's the loud thud of the trunk slamming shut, snuffing out the fresh air and leaving me alone and trapped in this tiny space.

An engine rumbles to life, and then we're moving, bouncing along a gravelly road that makes me grateful for the small mercy of the pillows.

It's the first, but not the last time I'm grateful for something my kidnapper grants me.

CHAPTER

3

I jostle against the pillows as the car bumps along uneven terrain, deep into the forest or up into the mountains, where no one will find me.

At least not until it's too late.

No one will start worrying until I don't show up at home in two weeks. And maybe even then, another week will go by before someone will notice something is wrong. That's the consequence of being a recluse, preferring to spend my vacation among mountains and trees instead of drinking cocktails with my girlfriends on the beach.

Whatever search will be conducted once someone realizes I've gone missing will be brief. This country won't care about a young woman who has gone into the mountains alone. They'll conclude that I've been eaten by a bear or fallen off a cliff. Another victim to Mother Nature. People die in these mountains every year.

That's when another terrifying thought strikes.

The Facebook post.

No one will even look for me here. Everyone thinks I went to Italy.

My breath speeds up to a frantic pace. The air crashes in and out of my mouth so quickly it doesn't reach my lungs. The darkness closes in around me, thick and oppressive. I frantically whip my head back and forth, trying to see anything, just a tiny dot of light.

Nothing.

Pitch-black nothingness swallows me up.

I shoot my hands up to rip at the bag over my head, but my wrists catch on the ropes. Struggling, I lift my legs and my head to get my hands closer to the bag, but the rope is too short. No matter how much I twist and turn, my hands remain stuck at waist level, never getting close to the fabric.

So I fumble for a hatch instead, scooting back and forth in the confined space, shoving my hands under the pillows, reaching as far up the edges as I can go. It's awkward and a hassle—especially when I search the inside of the lid and have to lift my back off the floor to reach it.

I'm balancing on my ass when the car hits a hard bump, and I crash into the side, bouncing off the pillows and hitting my head on the floor. I moan through the sharp burst of pain and curl up on my side as I accept defeat.

I'm not getting out of here until someone takes me out.

Hopelessness descends upon me anew, as dark and heavy as the blackness surrounding me. But just as I'm about to succumb to it, a little flicker of hope comes alight.

Nikolai. He doesn't have my Facebook. He took me to the train this evening, kissed me goodbye, and told me he looked forward to seeing me again. He saw me get on the train, and I told him I'd text him once I arrived in Brasov.

Will he worry when he doesn't receive that text? Will he even care enough?

I have no idea, but it's all I have. So I cling to the hope and let it be my beacon of light through the nightmare that has only just begun.

* * *

I'm bouncing on a hard shoulder again, my bound hands and legs flopping against a strong body after they cut the rope connecting them. The fresh air seeping through the hood brings me the scent of pine and wet dirt. It reminds me of Nikolai. And quiet hours spent hiking among the trees. But the scent does little to soothe me. Rather, it seems foreboding in my trussed-up state, witnessing a secluded place where my chances of rescue might be nil.

The bumpy ride has left me drained and sore. All fight is gone, my senses dulled after having been confined to the narrow space for God knows how long. All I can do as the bulky man carries me down a long flight of stairs is gasp and groan, stiffening my muscles to abate the bouncy movements.

A heavy door screeches, and the air becomes dry with a sort of dusty, old smell. The smell of stone walls.

Bright light of the artificial kind filters through the

hood, and the thudding steps of my captors become a loud echo as the sounds bounce off hard surfaces.

The acoustics change slightly as if we enter a smaller space, and then there's the clank of another hefty door.

Iron.

The bulky man places me on the ground, and then two sets of hands are on me, cutting off my clothes with mechanical proficiency.

My whole body is shaking once they're done. I want to cry out of sheer desperation, but I'm too numb, too stuck in the shock of it all.

"Get up," a gruff voice orders, and before I can even think to obey, someone jerks me up by the rope on my hands.

I stagger, barely able to find the strength to support my own weight. My tied feet are no help, and I sway from side to side when the man fastens my bound hands to something high above my head.

He cuts the rope on my neck and yanks the hood off. Sharp light assaults my eyes. Blinking, I catch glimpses of stone walls and ceilings from another era. Eerily old, but well-maintained. Two large figures loom in my periphery, and I try to focus my gaze to get a better look, but a jet of cold water throws my attention into chaos. I fall backward, wincing as the ropes strain around my wrists and icy coldness engulfs me.

I gasp to catch my breath and shuffle my feet to regain balance but never find it.

When the water stops, I'm hanging limply in the ropes. The painful bite into my wrists is nothing compared to the cold. It stabs at my skin and gnaws into my bones, and jerky shudders rip through my body and set my teeth chattering. I'm almost grateful when a set of calloused hands start soaping me up from head to toe. They travel over my skin in rough motions, making me feel cheap and worthless, but heating me nonetheless.

The small relief is brief, though. Soon, cold water splashes over my body anew, washing away the soap, the last few slivers of heat, and my dignity. Then the same rough hands pat me dry with a towel.

It's almost a relief when the other man pulls me into him, pressing my head to his chest and steadying me with an arm around my body, taking some of the weight off my bound hands. I have no idea what he's doing, but I almost don't care as I'm desperate for the heat he provides. I know that it's the same man from the train— the one who put the hood over my head, put me in the trunk, and told me to breathe. I know because he's less rough than the one who tied me up and soaped my body, his hands smoother, less mechanical.

The other one pinches the skin at the back of my neck, and I see a flash of something long and sharp in my peripheral vision just before it hits. A thick needle penetrating my skin. The prick is sudden and sharp, making me tense up in every sore muscle.

"No, no," is all I can say as pressure builds beneath my skin. "What are you doing?"

"ID chip," the man holding me says.

The other one picks up a scanner and holds it to my neck. There's a beep as it reads the chip. "245314," he says.

"Correct. Make sure it says she's off limits."

"Already done." The man behind me cuts the ropes on my wrists, and the other one hoists me up in his arms and carries me from the room. Once again, he holds me in his arms against his chest, almost like I'm human and not just a sack of potatoes.

I try to catch a glimpse of his features, but the harsh fluorescents are too bright. All I see are flashes of dark hair, more stone walls, and green iron doors.

It's not until he carries me through one of those doors and the light becomes softer that I can finally make him out.

He has a distinct longish face with a straight, prominent nose, long, low brows, and intense hazel eyes that make me feel like he can see directly into my soul with a single glance.

I have to avert my gaze when he looks down at me. It's like getting too close to the sun. But when he places me on a mattress in the corner, I can't help peering up at him again.

He's tall and lean, dressed in slacks and a black silk shirt with the sleeves rolled up to the elbows, revealing tanned arms covered in dark hair. He sports an upscale haircut and a short beard trimmed in even lines.

This guy definitely doesn't spend his days in a dark basement. He looks more like a businessman—a CEO of a profitable company.

"I'm Mikhail, but you'll call me Sir." He starts unbuttoning his shirt as he aims the magnetic power of his gaze at me. "You'll address every other man down here the same way. Are we clear?"

I curl up on the mattress and nod into my arms. It's

all I can do.

"What do you say?" he demands.

Humiliation wrenches at my gut as I mutter, "Yes, Sir."

The iron door creaks as someone comes in, speaking in a Romanian accent. "Where do you want these things?"

Mikhail must respond with a gesture because the door slams shut with a metallic clank a minute later, leaving me alone with my captor.

"Scoot over." Mikhail gives me a nudge as he lowers himself onto the mattress.

He doesn't need to ask twice. I turn around and huddle close to the stone wall, praying he will go away. At least, some part of me does. Another part can't stand the idea of being alone in this windowless prison cell, naked and shaking with cold.

A quick flicker of my gaze across the space tells me that's exactly what this is. A cell. There's a mattress, a toilet, a sink, and chains on the walls. That's it. I'm surprised the toilet is of the normal porcelain kind and not just a hole in the ground.

What surprises me even more is when Mikhail lies down behind me and covers us with a thick blanket.

I tense up so hard that my body stops shivering for a moment.

"Don't fight, *Koshechka*. We need to get you warmed up."

Then the strangest thing happens. This man, who has kidnapped me, stripped me of my dignity, and shoved me into a cold prison cell slides an arm under my neck, one over my waist, and gathers me to his now naked chest.

Warmth envelopes me on all sides, and the effect is instantaneous.

I can't control it, just like I haven't been able to control anything else that has happened to me on this horrible night.

A tear drips from my eyes, onto his arm. Another one falls onto the mattress, and then I'm weeping. I try to keep it down—I really do—but it doesn't work. Soon, I'm sniffling and jerking as sobs rack my body.

"Shh, *Koshechka*," he soothes, using the Russian endearment for kitten, as he slips a hand up to brush my wet hair out of my face. He doesn't say anything else, just holds me as I crumble under the force of it all. And God, I don't want to admit it, but with the way he strokes my arm and holds me tight, it almost feels safe.

It reminds me of Nikolai. His special brand of sadism mixed with comfort.

I hate myself for even thinking this monster is anything like the man who opened up my life to terrifying kinks and profound intimacy.

But the thought helps. The man behind me isn't quite as wide as Nikolai, but he's as tall, speaks in the same Russian accent, and seems to harbor the same contradictory characteristics. It's easy to imagine that it's Nikolai when I close my eyes.

My muscles begin to relax as I imagine Nikolai's arms wrap around me as he rocks me with gentle motions of his chest.

"That's it," my captor praises, and the smooth quality

of his accented voice is so much like Nikolai's that it's easy to disappear in the illusion.

But when his hand starts a slow trail down my stomach, unmistakably headed for my pussy, reality seeps back in.

"No," I pant, pushing against his other arm that is suddenly lodged around my chest with unbreakable strength. "No!" I repeat with more urgency as a long finger slides between my folds.

"An orgasm will help you relax—make your body heat up faster."

"I don't want one!" I shove at his hand, but he's already at my opening, feeling the cruel betrayal of my body covering my pussy in slick juices.

"Oh, but I think you do."

I let out a long, plaintive sound as he plunges a finger into me. The intrusion guts me, and the stark cruelty of my new reality wrenches at my chest when my eyes fly open. Bare stonewalls and a stranger who isn't Nikolai.

The illusion splinters like a thousand pieces of glass around me. I go frantic, writhing against his arm and kicking my bound legs.

"Hmm," he scoffs. "I thought you'd be more grateful. That's another thing to add to your training list."

I'm stunned when he removes his prodding finger, but then I see the manacles as he grabs the chain attached to the wall behind my head. Real iron manacles. They're not rusty and old—clearly not an original requisite of this old dungeon—but they fit right in.

The chain rattles as he moves the manacles onto my

chest, and my breath claws at my throat as it moves at a frantic speed.

Grabbing one of my wrists, he shuts a manacle around it. I try to fight, but as with everything else down here, it's hopeless. Soon, both my hands are trapped in the cold steel.

The manacles fit perfectly around my slender wrists. Snug enough to be inescapable and loose enough to not cut my circulation. The realization sends a jolt of icy fear through my veins.

But I don't get to linger on it for long as two fingers shove into my opening, easily sliding through my wetness.

"Noo!" I wail, bucking off the mattress, hating myself for being so wet—for allowing myself to disappear into the fantasy of Nikolai when my world crumbles around me.

"You should be grateful," my captor says, and the cruel edge in his voice has my eyes darting to him. "Only a few of the girls here get a free orgasm like this." He pumps his fingers harder, and even as pain flares in my lower belly, something tightens in my core. A heated sensation. An urge to go further.

"Why?" I croak, needing to distract myself from the shameful sensation.

"Because you're special," he says in his dark accent.

"I don't want to be special."

He lets out a nefarious chuckle. "No?" Climbing on top of me, he takes my cheeks in a hard grip while he keeps thrusting his fingers into me. "Would you rather I leave you alone in your cell, cold, scared, and horny?"

Horror rattles through my brain, messing with everything I thought I knew.

"Either you beg me for this orgasm, or I'll string you up from the ceiling and have Dorin flog you."

I stare back and forth between his eyes, trying to gauge whether he's bluffing.

He's not. I know it even before he says the next thing.

"I have two months to train you. I think that's enough time to mend the damage." He presses a finger to my forehead like he's talking about mental damage rather than physical.

"Please don't," I say, hating how weak I sound.

This man has me scared to the bone. Something about his sudden shift from protective caregiver to demanding captor is more frightening than if he'd been cruel all along.

"So, what do you say?" he prompts, his eyes flaring with sadistic power, already knowing he has won.

I squeeze my eyes shut, knowing it too. "Please let me come," I mutter so quietly I think he won't hear it over the slick sound of his fingers pumping between my legs.

"Again!" he demands with a force that has my eyes flying open. "Look at me while you beg me, and speak up."

I swallow hard and breathe through my nose as I try to calm the erratic panic stirring inside me.

"Please let me come," I blurt.

"Let me come, *what?*"

I close my eyes and steel myself with a long breath

before facing my own humiliation by staring into Mikhail's demanding eyes. "Please let me come..." I shudder and add the last word, "Sir."

A smile spreads across his features, crinkling the corners of his eyes and creating dimples in his cheeks. It should be utterly charming, but nothing will erase the sadistic cruelty that flickers deep in his dark eyes.

He pumps his fingers hard a few more times, and the unwelcome need grows inside me. But only a little, and the defeat thrumming throughout my system drowns it out. Not daring to go against him, I close my eyes and try to focus on the pleasure. But it doesn't work. There's no way this static finger-fucking will make me come.

I open my eyes and glance between him and the stone wall. "I—I can't come like this." I flinch as the words leave my mouth, expecting some kind of reproach.

One of his straight brows shoots up in an amused curve. "You thought I was trying to make you come like this? You really are an inexperienced little one, aren't you?"

I make a confused shake of my head. He's right—the wildest thing I did before Nikolai was the sixty-nine position. But how can he know? Does my sexual innocence linger on me like a stigma?

"Don't worry. We won't be able to say that once I'm through with you." He seems to muse on the words, and his tongue darts out to lick his lower lip as his eyes become unfocused for a moment. When he notices my confusion, he adds, "I'm just considering how I should start out." He studies my face as if searching for the answer there. "Maybe we should do it the easy way—get it over with so you can catch some sleep. You'll need your strength tomorrow."

Before I can respond, he leans forward and wraps his hand around my throat in a tight grip.

My eyes go wide with terror as the heel of his hand rests against my windpipe. He doesn't press, but the threat is right there, hovering, waiting to be released.

"Let's see if this will do the trick." He flexes his hand on my neck, gripping it harder, while he adjusts his hand in my pussy, angling two fingers upward and pressing his thumb to my clit.

Everything flips in the blink of an eye. Suddenly, my entire body pulses with need. And alarm. All he has to do is flick the right switch, and he knows just where to find it.

"Oh, yes." His expression lights up as he reads the effect in my wide eyes and clenching pussy.

"Please don't," I say, but the last word becomes a gasp as he moves his hand inside me, working his fingers against my g-spot and rubbing my clit.

Sensation shoots through my nerve endings with a force that sends me bucking off the mattress. He tightens his grip around my throat, just enough to let me feel the pressure on my windpipe without taking my breath.

It sends me straight back to Nikolai and the staggering orgasm he gave me as he choked me. It's the same deadly cocktail of fear and pleasure that has my world tilting on its axis now.

I fight the orgasm—try to keep my focus on my unforgiving surroundings. The nightmare that has consumed me in the blink of an eye. But it's no use.

Mikhail has already set it rolling, and my breaths speed up as tension coils through my body. All I can do is close my eyes and imagine Nikolai as pleasure shoots through my veins, pounds in my heart, and curls my toes.

A long cascade of moans erupts from my throat, deep and lustful. I jerk on the mattress and press my throat into the hand around my neck. All thoughts evaporate as I succumb to an orgasm as staggering as any of the ones Nikolai has given me.

"Hmm," a deep voice hums, and when I open my eyes, my world shatters once again.

There's no Nikolai. No bright sunlight. No scent of an earthy cologne. There's just my captor, the dusty scent of old rocks, and the four bare walls shutting me off from the world.

"That was easier than I thought." Mikhail gets up, cuts the ropes on my feet, and attaches manacles to my ankles. "No touching your cunt without permission." He tugs at my wrists to check if I can reach between my legs, and sure enough, they only reach my chest. "We'll fix something more comfortable tomorrow."

I don't even try to process his words. I just stare blankly at the ceiling as he puts his shirt back on, unable to cope with the twisted reality surrounding me.

Numbness has taken residence in my mind and body. I can barely think. It's nearly blissful, and I'm ready to shut my eyes and let sleep claim me in its restful arms when Mikhail is about to leave.

But the last thing he does breaks me again, spearing through the void and opening a crack to all the grief and desperation I can't bear to confront.

"I almost forgot." He shoves something plush under my arm, making the shackles rattle as he goes.

I stare down into the golden-rimmed eyes of a red teddy. The fox Nikolai gave me to comfort me whenever I feel lonely. The numbness draws back with a startling jerk, baring the raw emotions I blissfully ignored. My chest heaves under the weight, and tears well in my tired eyes.

The heavy door slides closed with a shrieky noise and makes a clank to cement the finality of my captivity.

Darkness descends upon me as the lights go out.

Left are only the hollow echoes of my sobs and the rattle of chains as I hug the teddy so hard it hurts and remember Nikolai's last words. A promise now squashed by these barren walls.

* * *

I glanced around the luxurious bar, feeling a bit self-conscious at the sight of the upscale clientele. Men in fitted suits, women in pretty dresses, and fancy cocktails being handed over the bar without thoughts about the growing bills. It was a scene that had always drawn me in. One teeming with control and power. And one I definitely didn't fit into. My soda alone had cost almost as much as my dinner. But despite my weeping credit card and my fidgety self-consciousness, I ventured into places like this every now and then in search of something. Something I could never quite seem to find. This night was no different, yet here I was, feeling close to that something.

Taking a sip of my Coke, I turned my head as someone

scooted onto the barstool beside me. I nearly choked on the soda as I came face to face with a bright set of blue eyes set in a strong face, staring straight at me. No, into me. Their directness was intimidating, yet the warm smile shimmering in them was disarming.

"Can I buy you another one of those?" he asked, nodding at my half-full glass as he pressed his palms to his thighs and turned on the stool to face me directly.

Setting my glass down, I swallowed the soda in my mouth a bit too hard. "Sure."

Taking my glass, he smelled the contents. "No alcohol, huh?"

"Hiking with a hangover is no fun," I said, tilting my chin a bit downward as a shy yet sort of heated sensation washed over me.

Lifting two fingers, he gestured to the bartender and pointed at my glass. The short reprieve from his heady attention allowed me a moment to collect myself, but the heady sensation returned the moment he locked eyes with me again.

"Hiking? Let me take a guess here. The Carpathians? You've left the flat fields of Denmark and come here in search of some mountains."

"How did you know?" I asked with half a smile, not quite knowing whether to be intimidated or impressed by his astute observation.

He huffed a laugh that had the faint lines around his eyes deepening. "Your accent is as flat as your country."

I just watched him for a moment. The almost boyish smile in his eyes. The lines on his forehead. The short stubble peppered along his strong jaw and the white streaks *at his temples.*

Christ, he had to be at least fifteen years older than me. I had just celebrated my twenty-fifth birthday last week, and he had to be at least forty. Mature and confident. And rich by the looks of his perfectly fitted suit and the massive watch on his right hand. He was a world away from me in every sense of the word. Generationally, geographically—judging from his Russian accent—and not least in terms of wealth and authority. I had just started my first job in a new city after having finished my studies last year, and I still felt green and uncertain in everything I did.

But despite the glaring contrasts, there I was, hopelessly attracted to this man I had only known for a few minutes, feeling some strange pull I couldn't put my finger on.

Maybe it was the warm smile in his eyes and those crinkles at the corners?

No, those weren't there when I first saw him and almost choked on my soda. It had to be the directness of those eyes. The way he held himself, commanding the very air around him without even trying.

"What is your name?" he asked, pulling me from my thoughts.

"Julie."

"Julie," he repeated, tasting the word. "Pretty name."

A shiver skittered up my arm as he reached for a pendant on my bracelet and his fingers grazed my skin.

"Is this your favorite animal?" he asked, toying with the small fox pendant—my favorite on the bracelet.

Biting my lower lip, I nodded.

"The little fox Julie is going into the woods," he said,

watching the silver fox with two golden stones as eyes. "All alone?" He directed his gaze back to me, still toying with the pendant.

I nodded, hoping he was asking what I thought he was.

"No boyfriend to keep you company?"

A bolt of anticipation had me shifting on the stool, and I gave a small shake of my head as I wetted my lips. "All alone," I confirmed.

Lifting a hand to twirl a lock of my auburn hair, he said softly, "A pretty little Lisichka going into the woods all alone."

"Lisj— Lisich—?" I said, trying to form the Russian-sounding word.

"Lisichka," he repeated. "It's Russian for little fox."

"Oh," was all I could say.

Releasing the pendant, he moved his thumb to my pulse point and circled with feather-light movement. "All alone in the woods, hoping the big bad wolf won't come to get her."

Something in his eyes darkened and deepened, and my breaths became shallow, my cheeks heating, as I felt something coming.

"Or hoping that it does." Leaning his elbow on the bar, he moved closer, and I completely lost the ability to breathe as he slowly slipped his fingers around my slender wrist, entrapping it in his strong grip.

My head clouded and the world around me swam as all I saw was him.

"Submissive?" he asked softly.

"What?" I all but gasped.

"I think you are," he said to himself. Tightening his

grip on my wrist, he tilted his head slightly as he studied my reaction. And that was it. I was spellbound. Unable to think or breathe on my own from that moment.

CHAPTER

4

I wake to the sound of screaming. The shrill wails of a desperate woman.

At first, I think it's a nightmare, or maybe a TV somewhere. The sound is too anguished to be real. I've never heard anything like it.

But as the noise approaches, the sound takes on a resonant quality a TV can't produce. It seems to bounce off walls and become even more obtrusive as a big, empty space prolongs the sound in horrid echoes.

No, this is not a TV. Someone is in real distress.

I jerk to sit up straight but fall back on the mattress with a thud as my arms catch on something. Something that rattles.

Chains, I realize. Chains connected to heavy weights around my wrists.

I fumble through the darkness, trying to make sense of it all. My hands slip over a thick blanket, onto a sheet that covers a foam mattress, and up onto rough, cold stone, where I find the attachment point for the chain.

I pull my hands away like I've been burned and clutch the teddy in my arms.

No! This is not real.

Closing my eyes, I try to conjure memories of my week with Nikolai—late nights of talking and laughing, fear and pleasure mixing together and exploding in earth-shattering orgasms, him holding me as I processed through tears. The promise to see each other again at the train station, the red fox, and finally getting on the train.

The train.

The memory gives rise to nightmarish images that flash before my inner eye and blend with the keening sounds in horrific harmony.

Except, it's no nightmare. The memories are as real as the screams that resound outside this dark space that is my cell.

Turning onto my side, I press one ear into the mattress and lift my chained hands to cover the other. It only takes the brunt of the sound, but I keep them there until the scream fades into the distance and finally dies with the loud clank of a heavy door.

Carefully, I lift my hand from my ear. The silence around me is jarring, and the sound of my shallow breaths adds a new layer of desperation as they become the only sound to fill the darkness.

I have no idea how long I lie there, frozen in place, my heart pounding with the speed and weight of a freight train.

Finally, I hear movement in the hall again. This time, there's no screaming. Just the clicking of shoes. Fancy shoes, I think, but the sound is foreboding, nonetheless.

The lights come on to confront me with the full vision of my situation, and then the green metal door squeaks as it slides open.

Holding my breath, I stare stiffly at the wall as the clicking steps approach behind me. A shadow moves at the edges of my vision, and a tall figure crouches by my feet to free my ankles from the shackles.

Then I'm confronted with Mikhail's deceptively polished face as he rolls me onto my back and shoves a key into each of the wrist manacles to free my arms too.

"Sit up," he orders in a clipped, business-like manner, and I get the feeling that he's neither here to toy with me or comfort me.

Gingerly folding my legs, I push up to sit, keeping the teddy firmly wrapped in my arms.

"How are you feeling?" Mikhail grabs my chin and turns my head from side to side as if inspecting an animal up for auction. "Any headache, fever, or"—he waves his free hand—"how do you say... nausea?"

I shake my head in his grip and train my eyes on the floor, where I see his shoes. Expensive ones, indeed. Brown, polished oxfords with decorative perforations.

"Good. Then we can get on with business."

"I need to pee," I say.

Grabbing me by the arm, he hauls me to my feet and points to the toilet. "Then pee."

I stare back and forth between him and the toilet, but he makes no sign of leaving or even turning around. "Can I please have some privacy?"

"No."

I gulp past the growing knot in my throat and sink

onto the toilet, burrowing my head in my hands as I empty my bladder.

Once I'm back on the mattress, Mikhail shoves a bowl of porridge into my hands. "Eat."

I lift the spoon and flatten my lips with disgust as thick, gray porridge drips from the steel.

"Kasha," Mikhail explains. "Very healthy."

"I'm not hungry," I say, having lost all appetite at the sight of the sticky mush.

He sinks to his haunches in front of me and levels me with an unforgiving glare. "Eat your kasha, or I'll have Dorin shove it down your throat."

I lift the spoon and try not to wince as I take it into my mouth. The porridge isn't as bad as it looks, but after eating half a bowl of the sticky stuff, it's hard not to feel a little sick at each mouthful. But I continue anyway, not daring to disobey. After all, I have a feeling that worse things are to come. *Pick your battles,* I guess.

"What is this place?" I ask as I eat. I already think I know, but I need to hear it even though the idea of hearing the words out loud scares me shitless.

"An old, forgotten castle, tucked deep into the woods where no one can see. Only people who are explicitly invited find this place."

"Someone must come here," I say, needing a bit of hope. "Hikers or people interested in historical buildings."

"Only if they're dumb enough to trespass. Even so, the few people dumb enough to explore have quickly gone again when they realized the place is inhabited, or because there's not much to see. Half the building was in ruins when I bought it. Quite unremarkable, really. Still is from the outside. But the dungeon"—he makes a chef's kiss—"just what I was looking for and in surprising condition. All I had to do down here was add a few upgrades." He rubs his scruff as he comes to think of something. "There was this couple who decided to explore further. I'm not sure how much they saw, but I wasn't taking any chances."

I gulp. "What happened to them?"

"Well, the man ended up in the incinerator, and the girl got her own private cell." He smiles as if he did her a favor, setting her up in a luxurious hotel room.

I shove the spoon into the remaining porridge, unable to get any more down as my stomach twists. "And then what?"

"I sold her to an Italian mobster. Made quite a lot of money on that one." He nods at the bowl in my hands. "Now eat up. I don't have time for this."

There are so many questions I want to ask, but I'm afraid the porridge will come right back up if I do. So I force the nagging worries away and finish the rest of the sticky mass.

Once I'm done, Mikhail sets the bowl on the floor and grabs my arm. "Let's go. Dax is waiting."

He leads me through the door and down a long wide corridor, around a corner, and into a room with a polished stone floor that feels smooth beneath my feet. But that's the only reassuring quality about the room. Except for the old stone walls, which are the same as all the other parts of this place, this might be a doctor's office. Cabinets line a wall along with a flat exam table, a large desk full of various equipment, documents, and a laptop stands to the side, and another exam table fills the center—or rather, a gynecologist's chair. Full of leather straps.

A beefy guy with long blond hair, who I suppose is Dax, greets Mikhail with a nod but doesn't spare me a glance. He's sitting on a rolling stool, his booted feet planted solidly on the ground, and his biceps bulge menacingly as he crosses his arms over his chest. My eyes trail to the snake tattoo that runs up the length of his left arm. I quickly look away again, afraid to provoke him by staring too hard.

"Get on the table," Mikhail orders, and when I shake my head and take a step back, the bulky guy gets up, grabs me by the waist, and hoists me onto it.

Shock locks me into place as he straps me down. My arms go into leather cuffs on each side of my head, my legs into stirrups, and a long belt across my belly has me gasping as he tightens it with a hard yank.

"I take it you want her rinsed out before we proceed?" the long-haired guy says with an American accent that has me turning my head. I guess I thought all men down here would be Romanian—or Russian like Mikhail.

The surprise snaps me out of the paralysis, and I start moving my arms and legs, testing the restraints.

No give.

So I fumble with my fingers to reach for the buckles on my wrists. But the leather is too wide, too tight for me to reach, and I pant with desperation as I strain my arms and back, lifting my head to see what's going on.

And that's when my composure snaps.

Dax, who has moved to sit between my legs and donned rubber gloves, is holding a huge syringe into a bowl, filling it with clear liquid. Maybe water.

I have no idea what he's doing; I just know I don't want that syringe anywhere near me. It's big enough to hold at least half a gallon. Its only forgiving feature is that it has no needle at the end.

"What are you doing?" I say in a shrill voice. I turn my head back and forth between Mikhail and Dax, begging with my eyes, seeking some kind of explanation.

For the first time since I entered the room, Dax looks straight at me. "Showing you that you no longer own your own body."

"No, no, no, no, no," I beg as he smears clear gel on the tip. The guy doesn't even flinch. He's cool composure incarnate as he drips a dollop of gel between my ass cheeks. Icy panic flares through my system at the cool feeling on *that* hole. "No one's ever touched me there," I squeak, fumbling blindly to find anything that will stop this guy from proceeding.

"I'm happy to be the first, sweetheart," he says without looking at me and presses a finger against my opening.

This can't be happening. It just can't. I squeeze my eyes shut to block it out, but the feeling of his prodding finger is too obtrusive. He's not even inside yet; he's just smearing lube around the rim, yet the sensation is devastating.

The finger leaves within seconds, but only to be replaced by a long thin tip that easily glides inside me, intruding upon my body in the worst kind of way.

"No, no, no, no," I chant as if the word could somehow erase this warped reality.

I clench and unclench my hands as my breaths stagger past my lips.

Then the strangest, most humiliating sensation of my life fills me. Water seeps in through my rear hole and fills my stomach.

Wrong. It's the only word I can find to describe it. Shameful, devastating wrongness.

I keep my eyes closed as I try to drift away to my happy place, surrounded by trees and bird song, a gentle breeze billowing through my hair. I succeed for a moment when the syringe disappears.

But then it returns, and more fluid seeps through that narrow canal, forcing all my attention to the sensitive place as more water fills my stomach unnaturally. Panic becomes nauseating flashes of neon colors in my mind, and I whip my head from side to side in a hopeless effort to expel the sensation.

"Relax, *Koshechka.*" A warm hand covers my forehead. Mikhail's hand. I'm not sure if it's meant to soothe or restrict, but it pulls my focus out of the alarming flares of red. "Breathe."

Opening my eyes, I stare into a magnetic gaze. There's no sympathy, but somehow, the compelling intensity I find there is enough to steady me.

I follow Mikhail's breaths, in and out, as water continues to distend my stomach. The fixed connection keeps me from crashing into panic, but the calm comes at a price. Because I can't hide anything as I stare at

Mikhail. All my emotions—pain, grief, and shame—are exposed in my watery eyes, my wincing features, and tiny whimpers.

When they finally unstrap me and lift me out of the chair, I feel raw and exposed. It's like one of those bad dreams where I'm walking down the street and suddenly realize I'm naked, and there's no place to hide.

I stagger on unsteady legs and cling to the two men as they lead me across the room. The water presses to get out, and I'm so focused on holding it in that I don't realize where we are going before they lower me onto a toilet in the far corner.

"This might take a while," the American guy says as he snaps a collar around my throat. The metal band is connected to pins sticking out from the wall, I realize to my horror, forcing me into an upright position when all I want to do is curl into a ball and hide.

I try to clench my ass and hold the water in to avoid the degradation of spilling it in front of these men, but I fail miserably. There's just too much water, and once again, I lose control over my situation.

The two men don't watch overtly but don't leave the room either. The American guy comes to check if I'm done several times, and when his patience runs dry, he simply presses down on my stomach, forcing the rest of the water out.

The shame knocks the wind out of me, and my legs are shaking, barely able to hold me up, when he shoves me into another corner and hoses me down.

My only consolation is that the water isn't cold.

"Do you want me to start training her ass?" Dax holds up a butt plug made of clean steel.

"I'll do it myself," Mikhail says, keeping his eyes trained on me as if I'm a flight risk.

But that's surely not the reason. I'm back in the chair, strapped down even tighter than before—two straps on each arm and leg and two over my torso. The only movement I can manage is wriggling my hands and feet and turning my head. Escape is as likely as trees growing out of the sky.

No, I think he's just bored, and I happen to be the most interesting thing in the room.

His gaze is unnerving, but it's not like I can do anything about it. It's not worth precious energy to fight right now. So I just lie there, shifting my gaze across the room as I try not to think about what Dax will do next as he puts the butt plug away and rummages to retrieve other items. I'm sure whatever it is won't be any better than the plug.

In the brief moments of shutting my eyes to my circumstance, I find a certain rest in the strict restriction. The tightness of my bonds dispels any thought of escape, and when I let my mind drift off to better places, the snug fit is almost comforting. Like a tight hug.

But then I open my eyes and remember that there are no good intentions in the bonds. They're meant to keep me still as the two men violate me, take away my most basic rights, and subject me to more degradations.

So I quickly snap out of the illusion and don't allow

myself more respites from this predicament, afraid it will only lead me back to that same warped place.

"The usual treatment? All gone?" Dax asks, snapping on new latex gloves.

"All gone," Mikhail confirms.

"All what?" I ask, speaking something beyond desperate pleas for the first time since Dax stuck the syringe into my ass.

"All hair." Mikhail takes a clipboard that Dax hands him and turns his bored gaze to the attached paper. "Well, everything but your wavy locks." Scanning the paper, he twirls a finger at the side of his head.

A small gush of relief eases the weight on my chest. My long auburn hair is one of my best features. Losing it would be like losing a fundamental part of my identity.

Dax rolls up between my legs on his stool and proceeds to smear hot wax on my private parts and rip off my hair with strips of fabric.

I wince and whimper through the pain, but I don't have much more reaction in me. If it had been last night, I would have been mortified to the point of a breakdown. But in the wake of the enema, waxing seems like a trivial matter.

Dax barely even looks at my face as he goes about removing every single hair on my body. I think I'm merely an object to him. Merchandise, like Mikhail called me.

It scares me. If I'm not a person to him, there are no limits to what he might subject me to.

But at this very moment, his clinical approach is a relief. I can almost pretend I'm at the doctor's, getting an exam.

Almost.

Mikhail disrupts the illusion with his authoritative presence that hovers close by. I constantly feel his gaze on me, and it makes me jittery and nervous. Like having a hungry wolf staring at you.

Apparently, I'm not the only one unnerved by his intense observation.

"You're freaking me out over there," Dax says at one point, glancing up from where he holds my ass cheeks spread to apply more wax. "Go shoot a deer or some cans, or whatever it is you do."

"Never mind me. Just do your magic." Mikhail takes a relaxed pose, spreading his legs to fill the space around him in that confident manner powerful men do. "Special delivery, this one."

"Aah, one of those." Dax goes back to work, and silence prevails until my pussy, ass, legs, and armpits are all free of hair.

"What else do you want?" Dax gets up and tosses the latex gloves aside.

Mikhail scans the paper on the clipboard as if it were a menu. "She needs birth control. I'm thinking an implant." His finger moves over the paper and stops as he speaks again. "A harness maybe. Cuffs. Or chastity belt. Something to keep her fingers from her pussy."

"Sure thing. I have a couple of options. How about piercings?"

I'm too preoccupied with trying to catch a glimpse of the items Dax retrieves to hear Mikhail's response. But he must have gestured to something on the board because

Dax gives a nod, saying, "Good choice."

My eyes dart back and forth between the men as if one of them is supposed to keep me updated. But neither one spares me a glance, and I forget about the piercing when Dax rolls a metal table with two needles up beside me.

One is small, one is huge.

When he frees my left arm, I immediately pull it down and grab onto the table as he flips up a flat armrest with straps.

Mikhail steps up to my side and easily pries my arm free, handing it to Dax. "Did you see the game last night?"

Dax huffs a laugh and inclines his head with incredulity. "You mean that thing you call football over here?" He presses my arm to the padded surface, and I jerk to get it back, but he's too strong. He barely puts in effort as he holds my flailing arm down with one hand and fastens two straps with the other. "I'd rather go golfing than watch that shit."

Mikhail makes some smart comeback, but I don't hear it. All my attention is on the needle coming straight for my arm. It's only a thin one, probably a local anesthetic—I know how inserting a contraceptive implant works. But it doesn't matter. I hate needles with an intensity verging on phobia, and I whimper pathetic pleas.

But neither of the men hears it, and the needle goes into my skin without a second's delay.

The sting isn't bad—really, I barely feel it. But the pounding panic in my chest is more than I can take, and when Dax lifts the big needle, I can't hold it in any longer.

"Stop!" I yell, filling the room with my desperate wail.

I expect them to at least pause their conversation and look my way, but Mikhail simply slaps a hand over my mouth to kill the noise as he says something about Liverpool, and Dax shoves the syringe into my arm, not even reacting to the sound.

It's only when Dax turns to clear the equipment away that Mikhail faces me.

"Relax, it doesn't hurt," he says, shaking his head like I'm a silly child.

My nostrils flare in time with my rapid breaths as I try to gain some modicum of control over the panic that's about to swallow me whole.

"Just a needle," he adds, releasing my mouth to slip his hand over my forehead, where he smooths away the hairs sticking to my damp skin.

I want to tell him that nothing is *just* a needle, but I'm too wound up—too shocked by their indifference—to say anything.

"Which way do you want to go with the no-touching thing?" Dax asks. "I could simply block the holes, but it might be better to restrict her hands, now with the piercing and all. I've had more than one girl ripping the wound when she tried to take it out."

Mikhail keeps stroking my hair with deceptive tenderness as he discusses ways to keep my hands from my pussy. Genuine or not, his touch keeps me calm. So I accept the small comfort, desperately needing it as they bounce words like chastity belt, butt plug, and muzzle back and forth.

When Mikhail removes his hand to go look at equipment, I feel lost. I stare at him as he stands at the other end of the room with his back to me, turning leather items in his hands and discussing something my ears don't register.

Again, I think it would be much easier if he'd let up the pretense of caring. It hurts too much when he walks away like he doesn't care. It hurts too much when I realize how lonely it is without him.

Without warning, tears spring to my eyes as I'm overcome by it all—the humiliation, the loneliness, the confusion.

I can't control it, and when Dax comes back to my side with a tray full of new items, tears are trailing down my cheeks, wetting my hair, and dripping onto the smooth leather surface. I want to lift my hands and swipe the moisture away, but my arms remain trapped, and the vulnerability shines bright on my face, baring my feelings in the same devastating way they've bared my body.

But as with everything else, Dax remains impassive, unaffected by my reaction. This time, though, it hurts more than I care to admit when he grabs my chin and looks me straight in my eye, seeing every little nuance of vulnerability on display there without showing a flicker of emotion. "Open your mouth," he says with the same clinical indifference he has displayed since he put me on his table.

I shake my head against his calloused hand. I have no idea what he intends to do; I just know I won't do it willingly.

And as with everything else, he doesn't need my cooperation. He simply digs his fingers into my jaw, sending jolts of pain through my bones until my jaw gives in to the pressure and goes slack. My mouth pops open, and he's quick to shove three digits inside, holding it wide ajar while he reaches for a device with two metal prongs that he shoves into my mouth.

He works the sidebar to make the prongs part, forcing my mouth open to the point where my jaw aches. The moment he retracts his fingers, I try to shove the thing out. But the metal is lodged behind my teeth, and there's no way for me to get it out.

A new surge of humiliation wrenches through my gut, making my stomach turn. I badly try to hide it, but I can't control the tears that trickle from my eyes, and with my hands bound, I can't even reach up to dry them off. I'm forced to lie there with all the despair and humiliation on full display.

I sniffle continuously, but soon snot trickles from my nose, and spit drips from my open mouth when I turn my head to hide the shame.

The air grows scarce in my lungs as helplessness becomes a vise around my chest. I heave to get in air, but none of it sticks. My hands clench and unclench at my sides as I whip my head from side to side, gasping for air and trying to process. I'm lurching straight for a panic attack, and I don't know how to stop it. Every time I move the slightest, some restrictive sensation reminds me of the nightmare I'm stuck in.

Wheels scrape against the polished stone floor as

Mikhail takes a stool and rolls up behind the exam table. Cupping my head between his hands, he aims his sharp stare at me, taking it all in. A pained whimper escapes me as he swipes at my spit-drenched chin.

"Do you have a sedative?" he asks, glancing up at Dax.

"Sure."

"Just enough to calm her down, nothing drastic."

"No!" I cry through my distended mouth as Dax retrieves a new syringe and disinfects the hollow of my arm.

"This will help you," Mikhail soothes, but his words don't register.

All I see is the needle coming straight for my arm. It sinks into my vein with the ease of a spoon in melted ice cream, and there's a slight pinch as Dax presses the butt, emptying the contents into my bloodstream.

The effect is instant. My vision blurs, and lethargy drapes over my body, making me sag in the restraints. A building scream dies in my throat as my head falls to the side, into the cradle of Mikhail's hand.

Blinking my heavy eyelids, I try to hone my focus on the calloused hands that pick up new items from the tray. It's all I can do. I can't even see which item he takes. I don't realize what it is until he clamps forceps around my tongue and pulls it out of my mouth.

Fear hovers somewhere at the back of my mind, potent and threatening. But it remains in the shadows, unable to penetrate the heavy blanket of fog that keeps my mind in a drowsy state of thoughtlessness. Not even when a thick needle approaches my tongue does the fear break free.

I vaguely register a hand moving over my hair, gentle and warm, coaxing me to let go. So I do just that. I let my heavy eyes fall shut and focus on the faint sensation—the calm heaviness weighing me down.

When a dull pain spears my tongue, all I manage is a small mewl. Then I slowly drift into a hazy place where nothing matters—nothing but the soothing hand and the floaty sensation.

CHAPTER

5

I come to in increments. Slowly, I become aware of my body. Tingling sensations prickle in my extremities and spread through my limbs as thoughts flicker through my mind with increasing vividness. But even as I wake, the fatigue lingers, bone-deep, and I think it's as much my system reeling from the time spent in Dax's chair as an aftereffect of the drug.

Vividness is not a welcome relief because with it comes physical and mental reminders of what happened in that chair—along with the realization of what the final violation entailed.

My tongue throbs as if someone has stabbed it. And that's exactly what happened. Horror infiltrates my dazed mind with oppressive black colors as I move my tongue and feel the click of metal against my teeth.

I wince as the swollen muscle throbs at the movement, and icy shivers race down my spine when comprehension settles into my mind.

A piercing. Solid metal through my tongue.

Why on earth?

Nipples, labia, clit, I would get. But in the mouth...

I can't come up with any plausible explanation, and the blank void scares me to the core.

The barbell feels entirely wrong. A constant violation in and of itself.

Instinctively, I lift my hand to touch the foreign object, but it's not skin that touches my lips. It's leather.

A foreboding sense chills me as I wriggle my fingers and find them locked in position.

My throat constricts with a growing lump as I hold up my hands to find them encased in black leather. But not just encased.

Trapped.

The gloves can't even classify as mittens since there's no separate room for the thumb. There's not even enough room to open my hand. It's two snug leather cases, keeping my hands fisted and useless.

I don't remember gloves. I barely even remember getting the piercing. All that pops up as I rack my brain is the sting of a needle in my inner elbow and a thick fog descending over my mind.

Closing my eyes, I try a little harder, and a few memories appear. But they're all clouded in a dreamlike mist. The forceps grabbing my tongue, the hand stroking my hair, and the sharp prick of a needle. Then there's the vague sensation of someone working on my hands and someone carrying me back here.

I open my eyes again and heave a shuddery breath. My hands look like two leather-bound stumps.

I can't take it.

Without warning, a furious energy surges through me. I jerk up to sit and shove one glove to my mouth, biting down on the wrist strap like a beast, uncaring of the sharp burn erupting in my tongue. I angle my head and bite and tug on the leather and the metal clasp, but nothing gives. The glove is locked in place. Even with a free hand, I wouldn't be able to remove it, I realize as I stare at the padlocks securing the buckle.

Still, I give it another go with the same result.

Staring at my leather-bound hands, I pant through my desperation. As my fury morphs into hopelessness, awareness seeps back into my body—into my pounding tongue. The pain becomes so acute that it spreads like poison through my veins and into my brain. I dart up off the mattress, seeking some kind of outlet for the pounding sensation lodged inside me.

And that's when I notice the chain. A thin, but solid metal band that connects the mittens to a collar around my neck.

A scream tears through my throat and bounces off the bare walls and back into my ears, mocking me with my confinement.

I rush to the door and bang on solid metal. With the leather providing a buffer for my hands, I manage to put in a staggering force that has the iron squeaking in its frame.

Suddenly, the door flies open. I stagger forward, nearly colliding with the mountain of a man who's opening it.

If I thought Dax was big, there are no words to describe this man. Not only is he tall, but wide and brawny too. His arms are like trunks, and his bulging chest looks as solid as the metal door. But that's not even the worst part. What has my blood running ice-cold is the menacing expression that is literally cut into his face in the form of a long scar that slices down one side of his mouth.

Before I can even think to apologize, the man has pulled a bundle of rope from his pocket and is shoving me back into the room. With a few quick motions, he loops the rope under my neck chain and ties it to a hook in the ceiling, forcing my hands and head up, making my back arch awkwardly.

I'm staggering in a precarious position when a thick stick connects with my ass. A scream tears through my throat as fire flares through my muscles, overriding any pain I felt in my tongue.

A hand catches me at my sternum, preventing my full weight from catching on the wrist-neck chain as I fly forward. It's a small mercy, but the tug on the collar is startling even so. And when another strike lands, I release a despairing wail that fills the space with a keening sound.

The strikes keep thudding into my muscles, sending me dangling in the chains and thrusting me deeper into blinding agony. I'm at the mercy of this beast of a man in every sense of the word. All I can do is scream and shuffle my feet in useless attempts at avoiding the heavy stick.

Tears are streaking down my cheeks when a voice breaks through the violence with a resonant power that demands instant obedience.

"Stop!" The clicking of square heels resounds through the empty space as the new man approaches.

"She kept banging on the door," the brutish man says, stepping aside.

"I'll take it from here," the new man says as long fingers wrap around my nape. He pulls my head back to make me stare up into a terrifying set of dark eyes under straight brows.

"Didn't get enough attention?" Mikhail gives me a shake. "Huh?" Glancing at the other man, he says, "Get me some lube."

Then he grips me around the throat and yanks me back into him, growling against my ear, "Maybe I should do this without, though? Teach you a lesson."

He slides a long finger between my ass cheeks, and panic flares in my already reeling body as he rubs a fingertip against my puckered hole.

"No, please don't," I beg, sniffling to control the effects of the tears.

"No? Why not?" He shoves a fingertip inside, and I cry out as his dry digit tugs at my tissues. He'll tear something if he goes any further without lube. And maybe he will anyway. I've never had anything up there—except the thin tip of the syringe.

"Please, I'll be good. I won't bang on the door again."

"No? Will you beg me to train your tight ass then?"

"No. Never," I whimper, more tears gushing from my eyes.

He moves his finger inside me, and hopeless indecision tightens my chest. No matter what I do, I'll lose. Either choice will tear at me—physically or mentally.

The brute returns and tosses Mikhail a tube.

"Last chance to beg," Mikhail growls, forcing his finger a bit farther in.

"Lube, lube, lube," I cry. "Please."

"Please what?"

I squeeze my eyes shut and force back my pride to save myself from agonizing pain. My voice is barely above a whisper when I finally manage the words. "Please use my ass."

"Not good enough." He smacks my ass hard enough to make me cry out and jerk around his finger. A raspy sensation like sandpaper scratches at my tissues.

"Please, train my ass. Sir. Please, Sir." The words crush me, and I break into a sob that opens the floodgates. Seeking purchase as desperation tears through me, I work my useless, leather-bound hands against the rope.

Mikhail lets out a cruel chuckle. "Since you ask so nicely, *Koshechka.*"

There's the sound of a lid popping open, and then cold lube trickles between my ass cheeks, around his finger. He pulls out and pushes in again, smearing lube onto the edges of my narrow opening.

He repeats a few times until he easily slides in and out, fucking my ass with his fingertip.

I feel dirty and vile, my ass smeared in sticky lube and a stranger's finger pumping into *that* hole.

"You're lucky I'm the first one to use your ass. If I'd let Dorin do it, you might not be so lucky to get lube and one digit at a time."

The bulky man huffs a cruel laugh. He remains at the

other end of the room, watching the violation unfold.

But I'm stuck on the first part of Mikhail's words. Nikolai should have been the first one to use me back there. More than once, he talked about how he looked forward to sinking into my tight ass, and I imagined how he'd carefully work me up to fit his size.

I weep, utterly broken. I weep from the indignity of it all, the devastating helplessness of losing my body, and the knowledge that Nikolai won't get to be the first one to use me back there.

Mikhail pushes a bit farther in, and my nerve endings spark to life, sending strange sensations into my tissues.

I hate it. I hate it so fucking much.

At least, that's what I try to convince myself of. But as he sinks a little deeper, I'm horrified to realize that my pussy is throbbing—begging for something to clutch onto.

"You're such a little ass slut. Did you know that?" Mikhail pumps in and out. He never sinks deeper than the second knuckle, but his finger is long, and the sensation is more than enough to shoot tiny bolts of electricity into my sensitive tissues. "You're fucking clenching my finger, begging for more."

"No, I'm not." I try to deny it ardently, but my body won't cooperate no matter how hard I try. The need keeps building until I'm desperate, crying then moaning, scraping the mittens furiously at the ropes, then arching my back.

"Do something about her pussy, will you?" Mikhail orders the brute—who must be Dorin. The massive man steps forward, unclipping his stick from his belt. It's as long as a police baton, but slightly thinner and rounded at the tip, and when he holds it between my legs, I realize it's to serve a double purpose.

I kick out a leg, trying to shove it away, but it only earns me a hard thwap on my thigh. Pain blossoms in my muscles, making me buck in the restraints, and he easily slides the stick through my wetness and pumps it into my pussy with a staggering force.

"Show me how much you love getting your holes filled," Mikhail orders with the same resonant authority as when he came in.

His words are vile and crude, but I can't deny the effect. God knows I try to, but he has already broken me down so much that there's nothing left to keep my defenses intact. So the command slips straight in, hitting into that perverted part of myself I've always tried to hide—always been ashamed of. It throbs and tightens deep in my belly, like Nikolai's commands have done all week, awakening a desperate need for release.

A moan bursts from deep within my stomach, and when he repeats the words, I come apart, writhing and jerking with the full force of an explosive orgasm.

* * *

When Mikhail takes me down and places me on the mattress, I'm numb. Shaking, but numb.

Both men leave, and I have no idea how long time passes before Mikhail returns with a steaming bowl of meat stew that he places beside the mattress.

"Eat," he says.

I don't move. I just stare into the space before me, feeling dirty and broken.

Worthless.

The slightest movement brings awareness to the sticky mess between my ass, a flicker of my gaze brings my attention to the black mittens, and any active thought takes me straight back to one out of the many horrors I've already endured here.

So I just lie there. Not thinking, not moving, barely even looking.

I feel Mikhail's eyes on me, studying me closely. When he sinks onto the mattress and grabs me by the waist, I instinctively whimper, expecting more pain or degradation. But he simply lifts me up to sit. Draping his left arm behind me, he uses it as a sling to hold me up as he takes the bowl in the same hand and picks up the spoon with the other. "Open your mouth."

I don't obey, of course.

"C'mon. Beef stew. Is good." He prods the spoon at my mouth, wetting my lips with the warm sauce, but I still don't open.

With a sigh, he sets the bowl aside and grabs me by the arms, turning me to face him.

"Look at me."

When I still don't react, he grabs my chin, and I finally meet his eyes.

"Good girl," he says with a slight glimmer in his expressive eyes. "Now, take a deep breath." Rounding his lips, he inhales deeply.

I take in a small suck of air that barely lifts my chest.

"You can do better." He slaps my stomach gently. "Deep into the belly."

He repeats the long inhale, and I find it's easier to obey his easy-going manner than it is to disobey it. After all, this order involves no humiliation or pain. So I take in a long, but staggered breath that reaches all the way through my lungs and into my stomach.

"Out again, slowly," he urges, and I push the air back out through rounded lips.

He has me repeating several times, and somewhere along the way, I start to regain my senses.

The moment I look away from Mikhail's steady eyes, harrowing memories flood my mind, and I start to draw back in on myself.

"No, no. You look at me." He immediately sees what happens, and when he takes my head between his hands and forces my attention back on him, the memories fade again. "Keep your eyes on me. Okay?"

I give a slow nod and let my attention linger on him.

Without breaking eye contact, he picks up the bowl and holds a spoonful to my lips. "Now eat."

Somehow, he manages to get me to eat the full bowl, keeping the devastating thoughts at bay with the sheer power of his gaze.

I wince as I move my sore, swollen tongue, and it takes me a while to get through the whole portion as I chew carefully.

The food isn't half bad. It's almost like a hearty portion of comfort food, and I feel somewhat revitalized when he sets the bowl aside.

My eyes drift over the room as if I've just woken,

and in a way, I guess I have.

But my surroundings are as bleak as before, making me long for sleep and ignorance.

"Do you need to pee?"

I take stock of my body and feel a pressure deep in my belly, so I nod.

Mikhail takes me by the waist, having the foresight to predict my weak legs as he helps me stand. A wave of dizziness hits me the moment I'm on my feet, and it takes me a minute to find my balance before I can move across the floor.

He helps me onto the toilet, then leans against the wall, looking bored as he waits for me to do my business.

I don't prolong the humiliation by begging him to leave, knowing very well he won't; I just look away and finish as quickly as I can. But the humiliations have no end today. When I reach for the toilet paper, I remember my immobile hands.

"I can't..." I steel myself with a deep breath. "I can't dry myself."

"Just drip. Someone will hose you down before bedtime."

I manage a few shakes before he hoists me back up on my feet and leads me back to the mattress.

Thinking he's finally about to leave, I curl up with my back to him.

But instead of hearing the heavy iron door, I hear the rustling sound of clothes and shoes being removed.

"I'm not cold," I say when he lays down behind me, naked from the waist up, and pulls the blanket over us. I am a little chilly, but I'd rather freeze than be stuck in this pretend intimacy with my captor.

"I know," he simply says and slides one arm under my head for me to use as a pillow while stroking my forehead with the other.

I tense up, trying not to lean too much into him. But my soul is starved for affection after what I've been through today, and somewhere along the way, my resistance lets up. Closing my eyes, I sink into him, and the man who has violated and humiliated me without a flicker of emotion actually hums as he gives me a tiny squeeze.

I stiffen for a second before breathing hard and asking on a long exhale, "Why are you doing this?"

"This?" He gives me another squeeze, tight this time.

I nod my head on his arm.

"I'm supposed to train you, not break you. And I came very close to doing the breaking today."

"And what do you care?" I try to pull away, but he simply bands an arm around my waist and drapes a leg over mine.

"Special client—makes you special."

"What's that supposed to mean?"

"A friend of mine has made a very specific order, and I'll train you to meet his demands."

I don't want to ask the question I already know the answer to, but I need to hear it. "So, you're selling me?"

"Yes."

His answer is a punch to the gut, and I squeeze my eyes shut as I try to breathe through the anxiety.

"No worries, *Koshechka*. You'll learn to like it. This is part of the request your new master made."

"That won't ever happen."

"I'm very good," he says with arrogant confidence.

Unable to bear more information about this sick business or have more arguments shot down with cold efficiency, I stay quiet.

CHAPTER

6

My days morph into a warped routine of constant humiliations, violations, and twisted moments of comfort in my captor's embrace. Time drags on at a dreadfully slow pace, and it's a struggle to keep count of the days. My only indicators of time are the artificial lights that seem to follow the pace of the day, coming on in the mornings and shutting off at night, and the three meals that seem to occur morning, afternoon, and evening.

Besides the trips down the hall to be washed in the evenings, I spend my days confined to my cell, hands in mittens and chained to the collar. Mikhail only frees my hands for a short while in the mornings, allowing me to eat my kasha and use the toilet, then again in the evening when I'm hosed down.

I've never been claustrophobic, but having my hands and arms trapped like this does things to my mind. I'll pace the small space of the cell until the soles of my feet hurt and the cold bites deep into them, then lie down on the mattress where I'll struggle to pull the blanket over me and try to lie still.

Moving around seems to be the only thing that will keep the panic at bay. When I lie down, it creeps up on me like a serpent, slithering around my chest and infiltrating my mind with terrifying images and thoughts.

So I shut my eyes and try to think myself away to a better place.

I think about the woods and the mountains I was supposed to hike in. The scent of pine trees, thick moss beneath my feet, and the sun glittering on a forest lake.

But then I remember where my last attempted hiking trip got me. The thick forest that seems to surround this place, holding out anyone who might try to find me.

I think about my friends back home instead, my cozy apartment, and reading a good book in bed.

But then I remember that I'll probably never see them, my apartment, or a good book again, and the terror slithers right back in.

The only thing that will bring me some kind of peace is thinking about Nikolai.

I imagine him holding me in his arms, peppering soft kisses over my hair, and rocking me with gentle movements of his chest. I imagine that he's the one who traps my arms against my chest while he fucks me. Sometimes, I'll even try to convince myself that it's his basement I'm locked up in and that it's all just a game.

But even as these thoughts provide momentary relief, they also stir up a wealth of shame and other harrowing emotions. Bringing this dungeon into my fantasy about Nikolai is like blasphemy, and I feel wrong and dirty every time I do. I shouldn't taint those beautiful memories with the sickness of this place. And I sure shouldn't get wet thinking about anything involving this place, but that's what happens whenever I think about Nikolai. So I try not to imagine that he's the one holding me trapped here, but sometimes everything is so bleak I need the escape no matter how wrong.

So I let myself go, imagining Nikolai coming down here, stringing me up to the ceiling and having his way with me. Spanking me, fucking me, and taking my breath. Sometimes he's sweet about it, sometimes rough. Either way, it always gets me soaking wet, and I find myself straining to reach between my legs. But the chain won't allow it.

It's almost a relief, not having to deal with the shame of rubbing myself to an orgasm in this place. But at the same time, it's a special kind of torture, not being able to find relief from the intense pounding at my core.

It feels like I've barely been here for a week when Mikhail discovers my dirty little secret.

I'm far off in dreamland, thinking about how Nikolai choked me and made me come, when Mikhail comes in with the second bowl of kasha of the day. He studies me with narrowed eyes as he sits down in front of me, about to remove the mittens. But he changes his mind, picks the bowl back up, and scoops up a spoonful of porridge that he holds to my mouth.

"Can I please eat on my own?" I ask.

"Open," he demands with a sharp tone.

Casting my eyes down, I part my lips, shame heating my cheeks as I succumb to another degradation. The only plus is that the embarrassment might hide the fact that my cheeks were already rosy when he came in. But I think he has already noticed. Every time I peer up at him, he has this look like he's privy to some dirty secret of mine.

Once the bowl is empty, he shoves the blanket in my lap aside. "Spread your legs." He slaps my thighs to make me open up for him, and I bite down on my molars as I see the stickiness glistening on my inner thighs.

Suspicion knits his brows as he pulls at my wrists to test how far down I can reach. But they don't go farther than my waist—not even when he bends me into an awkward position.

Grabbing my cheeks, he spears me with a stern look. "What have you been rubbing yourself on?"

"No—nothing," I stammer as fear rushes through me and collides with my embarrassment.

"Then why are you wet like a *shlyukha*?"

"I don't know."

He searches my face for an answer, and then a slow smile spreads across his features as he grabs the chain and tugs, making me jerk from the force. "You like this?"

"No," I deny.

He tugs a few more times, jerking me back and forth, easily taking control of my body.

Heat spreads to my core, sending more moisture between my legs. I can't help it—I simply can't. Being tied up and helpless has always been a fantasy of mine. Apparently, it doesn't matter how or with whom it happens.

I lower my head to hide the shame, but Mikhail won't allow it. Grabbing my chin, he forces me to face him as he gathers the chain links in his hand, pulling my hands up to the collar.

"Try to bring them back down," he challenges, and when I shake my head, he lowers his voice to a dangerous command. "Do it."

I give my wrists a tug. No give.

"Harder," he growls.

I try again, a little harder. When it still doesn't work, I put in more strength until livid energy pulsates through me as I jerk and writhe against his unbreakable grip.

I'm determined not to let him win, and I keep yanking until my breath is stuttering past my lips with heavy pants. Even so, I continue, pulling my legs out from under me to kick at him, twisting my lower body as I groan with the effort. But no matter what I do, my hands remain in place, caught by a single hand.

He just sits there, staring at me with hard eyes. Not even a bated breath reveals a little effort.

It's devastating. But as I keep struggling, the devastation morphs into something else. I'm not sure when or how the change happens, but when Mikhail moves his free hand between my legs to stroke my inner thighs, my skin hums beneath his touch.

"You like to struggle." He flicks a finger through my pussy lips, and I freeze on the mattress as I realize just how soaked I am. My breaths crash in and out through my mouth as I stare at him in horrified silence.

He slides his finger a bit farther in, and I can't help the moan that slips from my mouth. I press my lips shut as mortification tightens my muscles. But I lose control when he shoves two long digits straight into me.

"Aah." I buck over his hand as electricity shoots through my body.

He gives the chain a tug so hard that it shoves the air from my lungs—and feeds the pulsating sensations around his fingers.

He holds me dangerously close, his hot breath fanning my ear as he drags his fingers in and out at a maddeningly slow pace. "You know, most girls here would hate this. Right until the moment I break them. But you. You truly are special. You don't need no breaking to become a good little *shlyukha*." He lets out a groan that rumbles in my ear and sends shivers coursing down my spine. "Such a shame your hands are caught. You'd love to feel how hard my cock is."

I deny ardently with a headshake, but I'm not sure I mean it. I'm not sure about anything at this moment.

"No? Luckily, there's another way to find out."

With a sudden motion, he grabs me by the arms and flips me over. I gasp as I land stomach-down on the mattress with my head trapped in the vise of his hand around my nape. I flail my legs on each side of him as the scratch of a zipper intrudes upon my senses with a foreboding warning.

"Dorin," he calls out as he drags his hard length over my opening.

"Stop," I gasp, writhing to break the contact, panting louder with the knowledge that he's about to force himself upon me.

The creak of iron and heavy steps announce Dorin, and a crackle of violence thickens the air.

"Hold her head and lube her ass." Mikhail releases

my nape as a rough, calloused hand presses down on my head, pinning me in place.

Dorin must have come prepared. A second later, a plastic lid pops open, and I squirm at the horrible sensation of cold lube trickling down between my ass cheeks.

There's a swoosh in the air as Mikhail pulls off his belt. Lifting me by the waist, he makes quick work of strapping it around my hips—a simple harness that keeps me suspended. He hands it to Dorin and presses his huge erection against my pussy. I think he's going to push right in, but instead, he slides the head up and down between my slick lips, spreading my juices over my clit, taunting me with my own need.

Electricity crackles through my nerves, building and building until I'm bucking and moaning like a cat in heat.

A thumb at my ass has me going wild. "No, no, no!" I jerk against the strap and shove forward to break the mortifying connection. But I remain stuck—ass in the air, arms trapped under my chest, and head pinned to the mattress. Every tiny movement drives my helplessness deeper into my mind until it's all that exists. And fuck if it doesn't feed the crazed desire even more.

Mikhail holds his thumb at the edge for a while, letting me feel every little nuance of my defeat. And when he begins to rub the sensitive rim at my narrow opening, I can't resist the sudden burst of sensation.

My moans grow longer, my movements more jerky as the need to come blasts through my body with a force that threatens to burst something.

"Beg for my cock," Mikhail rasps. He pops the tip of

his thumb inside and holds it there as he rubs his full length back and forth against my other opening. I think he's struggling not to take me, and a thought flickers through my mind. *I could refuse just to let him suffer.*

But whatever little capacity to think I have left dies a quick death the moment he shoves the head of his cock inside, sending a maddening burst of sensation straight to my core.

"Do it," he demands, clamping a hand onto my hip.

Groaning, I push back, but his grip prevents even the slightest movement. I'm stuck in this torturous position, aching to feel the full length of him slide against my walls, filling me to the brim. There's only one thing I can do—only one thing that will put an end to this maddening desire. So I do just that. "Please, take me," I beg.

"Not good enough." He withdraws, removing both his cock and his thumb, and desperation has me hurling out the words he wants to hear without a shed of care for my dignity.

"Please, Sir, please fuck me. Please let me feel your cock."

"The bitch is learning," Dorin mocks, but all I hear is Mikhail's deep growl as he slams into me.

I let out a moan from deep within my stomach, but Dorin muffles the sound as he shoves my head deeper into the mattress. I gasp for air and push my head against his hand as I only manage a small breath through the side of my mouth. But Dorin only pushes harder, snuffing out my breath entirely as my head sinks into the mattress.

I don't know what's happening. I'm desperate and scared, writhing and struggling with panic, yet my desire keeps building with each futile jerk.

Mikhail positions his thumb at my ass, and I scream into the mattress as sensation bursts through my system, sending me straight to the edge.

"Come!" Mikhail demands as he shoves his thumb into my ass, and I convulse and jerk as I come apart in the most intense orgasm of my life. I scream into the mattress and buck so hard my legs lift into the air, leaving me suspended in the strap. Dorin eases the pressure just enough to let me draw in a sliver of air, and I keep screaming between staggered inhales.

Mikhail picks up speed, pounding into me so hard that he has me jerking back and forth against the belt. He grows painfully thick inside me, stretching my sensitive walls around him as he slams deep into me. I'm not sure if he prolongs my orgasm or sends me exploding into another. The pleasure keeps rolling, shooting through my nerves, sending my entire system into overdrive as I strain against the mittens, desperate for something to grab onto as he shoots his load inside me.

When he pulls out, I'm a sweaty, panting mess, jerking and twitching as the final currents of the orgasm settle down.

As the pleasure draws back, I become aware of other sensations in my body. The strap biting into my skin, the sharp ache in my twisted neck, and the fatigue. The burn in my tongue and in my ass. I wince as I adjust my legs on the mattress, trying to take some weight off the strap, and I push against Dorin's hand to turn my head. But I remain stuck, and claustrophobic panic creeps under my skin, clutching my lungs and infesting my brain.

"Please," I beg, but the mattress takes the word, and Dorin just presses harder, drowning my mouth in the foamy material. "Please," I repeat in a frail voice as I gasp for precious air.

"Leave," Mikhail orders, and I heave to access oxygen the moment Dorin releases my head. But the air won't reach my lungs. It just keeps dragging in and out of my mouth in shallow gasps.

"Take these off," I beg, struggling against the chains and the mittens as Mikhail rolls me onto my back. "I can't breathe."

Grabbing my jaw, he forces my attention to him. "Say the right words."

I scramble through the flaring red lights in my mind, searching for the right words. "Please, Sir," I blurt the moment I find them. "Please take them off, Sir."

A small smile tips up his lips. "Good girl. You *are* learning."

He makes quick work of unlocking the padlocks and unbuckling the mittens.

The moment I get my hands free, I roll onto my side, flopping my arms above my head as I drag in deep breaths that finally fill my lungs.

I feel Mikhail staring at me for a while, and then his hand moves to my back, drawing big circles. It feels slightly detached, like the comfort isn't quite genuine. But I don't care. I let the warmth of his hand seep into my frazzled nerves and let the motions lull me into a rhythm of deep breaths and empty thoughts.

***

The sexual abuse in my cell becomes another part of my daily routine. Some days, it's just fingers; some days, Mikhail will add a small butt plug; and sometimes, he'll let me have the full length of his cock. He may detach my hands from the collar and string me up to the ceiling, or he'll have Dorin come and hold me down—or simply do it himself.

The only constant is that he always makes me beg for whatever degradation he forces upon me and always tells me when to come. His timing is perfect, always giving me the order just as I'm about to fall over the edge, and I get a feeling that he's conditioning me. But I don't allow myself to linger on the idea. My mind is too full of shame, once Mikhail is through with me, to consider his motivations.

"Don't worry, *Koshechka*. You'll come to accept that this is who you are. A good little slut who loves to be subdued," he says one day when I begin to tense up under his comforting hand sometime after he has made me come. It's always like this. I accept his comfort as long as the post-orgasmic haze lingers, but once my brain clears up, I reject him.

"You'll have to break me for that to happen."

Grabbing me under the shoulders, he hauls me up to sit between his legs, pulling me back against his chest. The position is deceptively intimate, but there's no intention to comfort behind the gesture. This is to make his next task easier.

"We'll see about that." He drapes his legs over mine

and grabs one of my wrists in a steely grip, predicting my struggle. My obedience has vanished in the devastating defeat, and the moment he picks one of the mittens off the floor, I begin to writhe against him. It's not a conscious decision; it's instinct, knowing what panic will descend upon my mind when he encases my hands in leather and takes away my autonomy.

But my struggles are as useless as ever. It only takes Mikhail a minute to drag the leather over my hand and force my fingers into a constant fist.

"I won't ever accept this," I say in a hoarse voice as my chest constricts under the weight of the building claustrophobia. "You'll have to break me."

"Hm." He expels a half laugh. "Breaking someone is easier than rewiring their mind. Most clients don't care what they get—they just want a girl who'll spread her legs and open her mouth upon order—so I usually take the easy way. More profit. But even if you weren't a special order, I'm not sure I'd break you."

I shake my head and open my mouth to say something, but the sick depravity of his words has rendered me speechless.

"Because you, *Koshechka*,"—he grabs my chin to turn my face—"you don't need much rewiring. You just need to accept who you are and learn some manners." He releases my jaw to grab my other hand. "And a few tricks."

"It's never gonna happen." My voice breaks at the feeling of leather sliding onto my other hand.

"No? Just like you're not gonna lean into me and take my comfort in a minute?" He snaps the padlock shut, connecting the glove to the collar chain, trapping my hands.

I want to deny it, but all I can manage is a small shake of my head. I don't want to accept his comfort, but he always makes me. And with each time he does, his terrifying competence becomes a bit clearer to me, making me believe a little more in his promise to make me a good whore.

"Stretch your arms and open your hands." The taunting order is the same every time, and I whimper as I try to obey, knowing refusing is pointless.

The effect is instant. The moment I tug at my arms and the chain stops them, tears well in my eyes, and when I press my fingers against the leather in a fruitless effort to uncurl them, powerlessness drags me under.

"Harder," he commands.

I squeeze my eyes shut, my head falling forward in defeat as I tug with more force.

"No, no, no, you know how this works. Open your eyes." With a hand on my forehead, he pulls my head back, forcing me to watch the horrible sight of the leather-bound stumps of my hands.

The tears break free from my eyes as he has me struggling against the restraints twice more.

Finally, he lets off. "Good girl. Now close your eyes and relax." He smooths his hand over my forehead in soothing motions as he drapes an arm around my waist.

I try to fight it—I really do. The intimacy is a cruel joke after the things he's done to me. Tears stream from my eyes as I sniffle and whimper. I try to tense up and reject his touch, but as my grief grows, so does my need for comfort. Finally, I'm so broken I sink back into him and give in to the false safety of his touch. All I can do is hope he hasn't broken me for good this time.

CHAPTER
7

"Come with me," Mikhail says one day after lunch.

I only get out of the cell two times a day. To spend half an hour in a small fitness room with artificial sunlight and to get hosed down. I've already worked out today, and the cleaning usually happens after dinner, so I'm a bit tentative as I get up from the mattress.

Two weeks have passed. At least, so I think. My count got muddy somewhere after the first week, and it gets harder by the day to keep track in this static blur of gray walls and humiliations.

He waves a hand at me, silently urging me on, and I pad across the cold stone floor. Instinctively, I step close to him like he's my shelter that will protect me from whatever is outside the green metal door, and I scold myself inwardly and take a step away.

I've grown more pliant during the last few days, willingly giving him my hands when he puts the mittens back on, and my begging for orgasms comes more readily.

I tell myself it's because I'm depleted and don't have the energy to fight, but really, I think it's because his training is working. I can tell by the way his order to come usually pushes me over the edge even before I'm at the precipice. It scares me to the core, and I tell myself I'll be more aware of his conditioning and fight it the next time. But it never works. He always shuts my brain off expertly, so I never realize what's happening before it's too late.

Instead of grabbing me by the arm and hauling me along, he simply presses a hand to the small of my back. And that's all he needs. I compliantly go along as he guides me through the barren halls.

But when he opens the door to Dax's room of hell, I freeze in place. Cold fear washes over me as I click my tongue piercing against my teeth and remember the horrible sensation of having my stomach pumped full of water.

"Get on the table." Mikhail pushes me inside, and I'm not sure if he actually expects me to obey or just leaves the problem up to Dax. Either way, I don't move as he turns to Dax. "I'll be back in a minute. Start without me."

Then he's gone, leaving the door half ajar, me standing frozen in place as I watch Dax go about preparing whatever degradation he has in store for me.

At first, I only catch a few glimpses of his rolling table behind his broad frame. But when he steps aside to fill a bowl with water, I get the full view.

Lube, latex gloves, and the huge syringe with the long plastic tip that went in my ass.

Panic takes me in a chokehold. Everything within me

freezes like it's a sedative and not adrenaline that has invaded my veins. All I can move are my eyes, and I dart them across the space like it could alleviate the icy fear. But all it does is aggravate the paralyzing powerlessness as I see the many straps on the table, the stirrups, and the metal collar jutting out from the wall by the toilet. And finally, my own leather-bound hands.

Dax places the bowl on the tray and turns to me, retrieving a key from his pocket. Without granting me the humanity of eye contact, he starts working on the mittens. He unlocks the padlock, frees my hands, and removes the collar, leaving me stark naked.

Then he turns to put it all aside and rolls the table up beside the gynecologist's chair. "Hop on." He pats the smooth leather surface, still not bothering to look at me.

I stare down at my free hands, flicker my gaze to the table, then back to the open door. Being free from the gloves is like a rush of fresh air—a breath of hope. It knocks me from my paralysis and into action.

What I do next is not a conscious choice or a thought-through plan. It just happens. Instinct kicking in.

Three careful steps are all it takes to bring me out of the room without Dax noticing.

And then I bolt.

I dart down the empty corridor, driven by a sharp burst of adrenaline. I barely even feel the hard stone beneath my feet or the strain in my legs. I just run.

I'm almost at the end, where the hall splits in a T, when I hear Dax's angry voice behind me. His words don't register; I only hear the boom of his voice rip through the tunnel-like space. Then the thudding sound of hastened steps. When I veer around the corner and glance back, I'm stunned to find he's not running.

Fear pulses through my veins as I realize there might not be a way out. Still, I keep going, my bare feet pounding against rough stone as my pulse becomes a jackhammer in my ears. Panic is a violent kick in my beating heart when I reach a closed metal door, more solid than the green cell doors, at the end of the hall. I frantically try the handle. Locked. My eyes dart up and down to assess what I know in my gut is an exit. There's not even a lock under the handle, only a digital plate beside the door, and that small plate shoots more terror through my veins.

I shove my hand against it. A finger. Bang on it.

Nothing.

Panic spurs me on—down a new corridor full of green doors like the one on my cell. I grab the first handle I see and the next. But they're all locked. I keep yanking at handles, glancing over my shoulder. Still no Dax.

A shrill scream somewhere jolts my feet back into action. I bolt toward the end and down a new corridor. I keep running, trying handles. Steps echo somewhere in the distance, another scream, then steps from a different direction.

I veer to the left, then right, right then left. I have no idea whether I'm moving in circles. I just try to get away from the sounds.

Everything looks the same until it doesn't.

I veer around a new corner, and everything changes in an instant. A gust of chilly air sends shivers down my spine, and my feet ache against the gravelly floor as I stare into thick darkness.

My eyes dart around, trying to gauge my surroundings.

A tendril of fear slithers down my spine when I catch a glimpse of old bars instead of a door, and I gasp in shock when my feet hit something hard and long. With my heart pounding in my throat, I stop running and continue at a more careful speed.

With two more turns, the darkness becomes so thick I can't see my own hands. I halt and turn around, searching for something—anything to guide my way. But there's no flicker of light. I'm caught in stifling blackness.

I reach out for the wall, hoping it will guide me back. But I can't reach it.

Fear bands around my lungs as I keep whirling around without seeing or touching anything.

Shudders take over my body—a violent mix of fear, exhaustion, and waning adrenaline. I sink to the ground and curl my knees up to my chest as tears start dripping from my eyes. I turn my head every other second, thinking I hear something, and flicker my eyes back and forth, thinking I see a shadow.

But the darkness remains dead-still and empty.

I'm alone. All on my own and more scared than I've ever been in my whole life. More scared than when Mikhail propped pillows around me and shut me into the darkness of the trunk. At least then I knew where I was— I could feel my surroundings. They were small and comprehensible. Here, I have no clue what lurks in the corners or even where the corners are. I feel like I'm drowning in dead darkness.

All I have are my own bated breaths and my tiny whimpers that become ominous sounds that barely sound like my own as they blend into the nothingness.

I rub my arms, my legs, and my feet to abate the cold. But eventually, it seeps through my skin, into my bones, where it shakes me to the core.

It feels like I sit there forever, but I'm not sure it's even an hour.

When I finally do hear steps echoing through the empty halls nearby, I'm more relieved than scared. Right now, I don't care about who finds me or what the consequences will be; I just want to get out of this black, cold hole.

Light flashes, and I squint as I gaze up at the tall figure approaching me. When I make out Mikhail's straight and low brows, I'm so grateful I crawl toward him.

"I'm sorry." I feel godawful pathetic as I sniffle and lean into his leg. But I'm unable to stop myself.

Mikhail grabs me by the hair and yanks me up, and I don't even protest at the pain exploding at the back of my head. I just want to feel him close—know that I'm not alone.

The full weight of my captivity must have caught up to me, snapped around my neck like an iron manacle, and made me into this person who seeks her captor's touch out of want for better.

I take it without a modicum of self-respect.

I curl my hand around his shirt as I weep, desperately trying to draw closer—to burrow my head in his chest and seek his comfort.

But he doesn't offer me any, and the rejection hurts more than any other thing he's done to me.

He tightens his grip on my neck and shoves me forward, through the blackness and back into the long corridors. Somehow, the light restores some of my strength, and I manage to get enough of a hold on myself to stop the tears and let go of Mikhail. But the pain of his cold distance remains.

"It's time for the chair," he announces when Dax approaches us from the other end of a hall.

Dax's mouth curves up in a wide, wicked smile—the type of smile that belongs to a charming surfer guy on the beach in summer.

But it looks cruel down here, and when Mikhail shoves me into a new room, I know why.

In the middle of it all, a large wooden structure that looks terribly much like a death chair rises on a small platform.

I push back against Mikhail's arm, shaking my head with the full force of my desperation.

"Don't worry, sweetheart, it's not what it looks like," Dax says, stepping up to the chair and tapping the back like it's an old friend. "I've built this one for a whole other purpose."

"Sit." Mikhail's voice booms through the room, shocking me into action.

I scurry across the cold floor and scamper onto the chair. It's so tall I have to use my arms to hoist myself up. It's not until I'm seated on the wood, feeling like a child in a grown-up's chair, that I realize there's a hole in the middle of the seat. But my attention quickly snaps back to Mikhail.

"Use the hood," he says, staring me down as he talks to Dax. "If she wants to be alone, she'll goddamn get to be alone. The ear muffs too."

I shake my head wildly. "I don't want to be alone."

Mikhail doesn't react, and I'm about to jump out of the chair to go beg him when Dax drags a leather strap over my stomach, through a vertical slit in the chair's back, and pulls.

The leather forces me back against the wooden surface as he buckles it in place. Panic sends me into frantic motions, tugging at the strap, wriggling my hips, and throwing my hands back in search of the buckle. But the wooden back is too wide, the slit too narrow to get my fingers through. There's no way for me to reach it.

I'm trapped, well and good, by one simple belt.

But Dax doesn't do simple. He proceeds to strap my arms and legs down in several places, forcing my legs wide open and pinning my arms to the armrests, my torso to the back.

When he tightens a final strap over my waist, I can't move anything but my head. But I don't think that's going to last long either as I catch a glimpse of leather straps appearing through slits on either side of my neck.

I cast Mikhail a final pleading look, but he just stands there with his hands folded in front of him, legs wide, as he watches me with a cold expression. Like an executioner.

A bag comes over my head and shuts me into claustrophobic darkness. I whip my head from side to side, clutching my hands around the edges of the armrests.

"I'm sorry," I whimper, and the worst part is that I truly am. "Please, Mikhail—please, Sir. Don't do this."

Leather closes over my neck, pulling the bag close around my head.

"No!" I wail as another strap comes over my forehead.

But no one hears my pleas. No one cares.

And then my world becomes a narrow tunnel of despairing wails and whimpers as ear muffs shut out every sound but my own.

* * *

Panic slithers through me. A thousand tiny snakes coiling around my lungs and creeping under my skin.

I've stopped begging, unable to stand the sound of my own desperation. Now it's just my frantic breaths sounding in my head like a scene from a horror movie where the girl steals through the woods, not knowing the monster is right behind her.

It's even worse than the harrowing blackness of the old halls I got myself trapped in.

I startle when something or someone brushes against my thigh, and my yelp resounds in my ears as loud as the scream when the monster catches the girl. Then something is at my pussy—at the hole in the seat of the chair. Fingers smear something sticky between my folds. Lube. The quick, effective motion tells me it's Dax. He doesn't see me—never does. No lingering glances on my breasts or lingering touches on my private parts. To him, I'm a machine getting oiled and ready for use.

With the darkness of the old halls having sucked out my strength, I can't uphold my sense of worth. I slump in the restraints and whimper as my mind wipes out my dignity. A painful jerk tears at my body as another touch startles me. This time, it's inanimate. A toy of some sort prodding against my opening, sending me deeper into the dehumanized state. I'm not even worth human touch anymore.

My inner muscles contract to reject the object, but the slick lube allows free entrance, and what appears to be a thick dildo sinks into me, spearing me with the knowledge that my body is no longer mine. The toy just sits there, horrible and obtrusive, as Dax proceeds to smear more lube onto my clit and press a new object against it, which he seems to attach to the chair.

I sense him step away, and I give a slight jerk of my hips, hoping to dislodge the unwelcome thing. But I barely have an inch of leeway, and even so, the thing doesn't budge the slightest. All I achieve is to press myself a smidgen farther into it.

A sudden buzzing against my clit sends a painful shock through me, and my yelp is a loud sound in the hollow void. Another shrill sound rings in my ears as the dildo starts moving inside me. It drags along my inner walls, almost all the way out, then slides back in to hit the bottom of my pelvis. Then it goes back out and in again at the same measured speed. It's a machine, I realize; not a man controlling it.

I squeeze my eyes shut with the effort of trying to drown out the sensations. But my mind doesn't have the strength to take me someplace else, and my body reacts without need for permission. Tingling sensations erupt in my sensitive skin as the buzzing keeps going, and my inner walls twitch around the vile intrusion, wanting to grab onto it and welcome it in.

Somehow, I must not be broken entirely because I muster just enough strength to hold it together—hold back the moans and the urge to let the buzzing sensation drag my body into lustful need. But my stamina only lasts so long.

The dildo keeps going, in and out, in and out, and the vibrator keeps buzzing. It seems to go on forever, and finally, my last sliver of mental strength wanes, and my body takes over.

At first, it's tiny mewls that fill the empty space inside my head, and the tingling sensations spread through my lower body. Then the mewls turn into tiny moans as the tingles become little bolts of electricity that have me jerking against the straps. And finally, the sensations take over my whole system. Long, desperate moans fill the lonely silence, and cold sweat breaks out over my skin as I clench my muscles around the maddening intrusion and spasm under the constant buzzing.

My entire body convulses with the need for release, but the humming vibrations and languid movements of the dildo don't cut it. It's not enough to send me over. But it's too much to allow me to forget.

It keeps going at the same torturous pace in one

cruel loop—in and out, in and out, buzzing at a constant low—until I'm teetering on the edge of insanity.

"Please, I ca—I can't... take anymore." My voice sounds shaky and frail to my ears, and I hardly recognize it. I don't recognize myself.

No one answers, and I try again a little louder.

"Please, stop. I—I'm sorry. I won't ever run off again. I promise." My voice breaks on the last words. No one but myself hears, and I can't bear the broken sound. I can't bear to be in this body that's not mine anymore. I can't bear the cold, empty loneliness.

Tears break from my eyes, and hoarse whimpers erupt from my throat. I try to stop it, but this is just another thing I have no control over. The whimpers turn into sobs, and my world becomes steeped in agony as my grief is the only thing I hear, the painful pulsations in my body the only thing I feel.

Sniffling, I try to keep control over one last thing, but it's no use. Soon, my nose is running, and snot and tears wet the enclosed confines of the bag, draping me in more lonely humiliation.

I can't take it. I just can't. Desperation builds inside my head, threatening to explode. I jerk against the restraints, fueled by blinding panic.

"Let me go!" I wail, only for my own ears to hear. But I can't stop even though the desperation drives me deeper into the panic. "Let me go. I can't take it. Stop!"

My world blurs as I teeter on the edge of something. A breaking point? Unconsciousness? I don't know. I just know that something's about to snap.

And then it all ends.

The vibrations cease, and the dildo goes still inside me.

My screams die, leaving my breaths an echoing sound in the stillness as I wait for something to happen. But nothing does. I just sit there, breathing hard and reeling as my entire body aches from the intensity of everything.

At some point, I let go of the fear and let the stillness claim me into some sort of warped rest. Everything is hollow and empty, and my body becomes a dull weight that is there yet not quite mine to feel as I sink into the darkness.

My breathing is calm and my mind the same when my world is suddenly thrust back into a state of alarm.

The buzzing begins with a force that shoots an overload of sensation into my sensitive nub, and the dildo begins at a hazardous pace that has a screech like a demon's wail clawing up my throat.

I jerk and strain against the straps, the wood, and the buzzing toy, but there's nothing I can do to escape the onslaught of sensation. Nothing but scream and claw my fingers against the wooden armrests.

The sensations are like fireworks gone wrong in my nerves, and the jolts are painful as they rip through my body. But slowly, they coalesce. My core starts humming, drawing the energy toward my center. It all gathers low in my belly, pulsing and contracting with an intensity that nearly has me fainting. My moans deepen, and my toes curl. I'm just about to come when it all ends.

Just like that.

The buzzing stops and the dildo draws out

completely.

Cold, aching emptiness slithers through my veins, and I wail like a child.

I can't take it anymore. Not the loneliness, the aching desire, or the strain in my body. There's simply no energy left.

Yet somehow, I go through the same violent turbulence of cruel sensation and terrible emptiness three more times.

When the dildo draws out and the buzzing stops for the last time, I don't even scream. Not a sound moves past my lips, and it feels like a miracle that my lungs will work to take in air.

My skin is damp and sticky, my mouth dry and scratchy. All my joints and muscles hurt, and pins and needles stab against my skull.

A gust of air has my breath catching from the shock. I haven't felt anyone's presence for a very long time, and knowing someone is close is as unsettling as it's reassuring.

The ear muffs disappear, and the relief of hearing something beyond my own wails and whimpers is so great that I start weeping again. I barely make any sounds, but the tears keep trickling down my face behind the bag.

Someone leans close, and a hot breath seeps through the fabric against my ear. "Are you gonna be a good girl tomorrow and get on Dax's table so he can clean out your ass?"

The constriction around my lungs eases at the sound of Mikhail's voice, and I feel like I can breathe again for the first time since Dax put the bag over my head.

"Yes," I say without hesitance, though there's barely any sound in my voice.

"What's that?" Long fingers trail along my collarbone, and I ache to reach out and touch him—to feel that he's truly there and it's not just an illusion my burned-out brain conjures. I need to find out if he's mad or he has forgiven me for running off.

"Yes, Sir," I manage with more clarity.

He moves away, and the loss is as painful as the denial of the last orgasm.

"Take her out," Mikhail says, and a minute later, rough hands are working on the straps.

Mikhail is gone when I finally get the hood off. It's just Dax and me.

My muscles are so weak I don't think I can stand, and I sag against the wood when he loosens the strap around my neck, not even making an effort to get up when he releases the final one around my chest.

Dax hoists me over his shoulder and carries me to the washing room, where he makes quick work of soaping me up and hosing me down. Then he takes me back to my cell, where he dumps me on the mattress and puts manacles on my hands and legs before leaving me alone in the darkness.

CHAPTER

8

I feel terrible the next morning.

Not because of the strain in my body—well, that too—but mostly because of the gnawing guilt.

I shouldn't feel guilty about anything down here. But no matter how much I try to rationalize the guilt away, the message won't stick.

Somehow, Mikhail has bent me so much to his will that obedience is taking precedence and wiping out my natural instincts. I don't know if it's been coming for a long time or if something snapped in me when I was in the chair yesterday.

It doesn't matter. The need to obey is there, blaring and loud.

He clearly senses it too. He lets me eat the kasha on my own in the morning, leaving the cell while I do, and when he returns, I'm on my knees, hands flat on my thighs and head bowed. "I'm sorry, Sir," I say when his perforated shoes appear before me.

"Finally getting somewhere," he says with a

disgruntled edge, like he's still mad at me for running.

I hate it, hearing the disappointment in his voice. Lifting my head, I face his hard expression. "I'm really sorry, Sir," I say, my mouth twitching as emotions threaten to spill.

He peruses me for a moment, then lets out a grunt as if accepting my apology. "Are you going to behave today and let Dax clean you out without a fuss?"

Inhaling a staggered breath, I look down and nod.

"Don't forget what you learned yesterday, or I'll have to teach you again," he scolds.

Leveling myself with another deep breath, I look up. "Yes, Sir."

He accepts with a brusque nod and opens the door. "Then crawl to Dax. Hands and knees."

I crawl down the empty hall, my head lowered in submission and my movements slow and measured. Mikhail follows two steps behind, clearly testing my obedience. I deliver in every way possible. I don't even think about running, and not even when a guard passes with a struggling girl do I look up. All I see is her kicking legs in my peripheral vision as he carries her in front of him. It's eerie because she doesn't make a single sound. All I hear is the heavy thuds of the guard's boots.

"Can I ask a question?" I say once they have passed.

"Go ahead," Mikhail replies. "As long as you keep moving."

"What happened to her?"

"Dax cut her vocal cords."

I go stiff in all muscles, clenching my teeth as horror washes over me. Yet I keep crawling.

Grabbing my hair, Mikhail stops me and leans down to face me. "He's not gonna do that to you."

I stare at him with wide, horrified eyes.

"Okay?" he asks.

"Okay," I parrot with a slight nod.

"He only does that upon order. Most men like to hear their women scream, but a few enjoy the silence." He releases my hair and straightens. "Or the power of taking their voice." With a soft kick to my ass, he spurs me on. "Now, keep going. Dax is waiting."

I continue on my hands and knees and veer to my left, through an open door, when Mikhail gives the order. I stop just inside, my heart pulsing wildly from what Mikhail just told me and from the sight of Dax's office. With my head down, I don't see much, but the clinical metal of the rolling table and the gynecologist's chair is more than enough to tell me where I am.

"The chair worked?" Dax asks.

"Seems like it," Mikhail replies and kicks my ass again. "Get on the table."

I rise to my feet, keeping my head down to avoid facing Dax as I scoot onto the table, perching on the edge, between the stirrups.

"Well, that's a change if I've ever seen one." Dax steps between the stirrups, right in front of me, and grabs my chin. For the first time, he looks me straight in my eyes as he lifts my head. His face remains impassive, giving nothing away, but his eyes roam across my features like he has found something new that has caught his curiosity.

"Lie down," he says, releasing me and taking a step

back.

Pressing my hands to the edges, I gingerly move farther in and lean back, staring into the ceiling as the heavy weight of my situation settles over me. I've just willingly placed myself in this chair, all but abetting the abuse and degradation Dax is about to thrust upon me. I can't take it, but I can't fight either. So I shut my eyes and squeeze my fists at my sides as I try to breathe through the tight constriction in my chest.

"Give me your left hand," Dax says as he steps around the table.

I lift my hand and let him bring it above my head and place it in one of the attached leather cuffs. The leather wraps around my wrist as Dax pushes the strap through the buckle, and I jump as he pulls tight to close it. Then he does the same to my other hand, and I obediently go along, letting him trap me deeper in helplessness, letting him chip away at my autonomy. All without a peep.

"Pull at your hands," Mikhail says once both are trapped in the cuffs.

Opening my eyes, I face him, wanting to protest, but as he keeps staring me down with uncompromising authority, I relent. First, I give a little pull, and when he lifts his eyebrows, I pull harder until I'm jerking at the restraints, moaning and whimpering at the unbreakable resistance. Heat swirls in my core even as embarrassment and defeat coil tight inside me.

"Enough," Mikhail says, and I go still, gluing my eyes to the ceiling as I bite my lip to suppress the gnawing defeat.

Silence prevails for a whole minute, and when I glance toward the two men to see what's going on, I find Dax watching me with a strange sort of fascination, head slightly tilted.

A smile spreads across his lips as he points at me and looks at Mikhail. "Did that turn her on?"

"Sure did."

"Well, well, well." He makes a slight tilt of his chin and steps between my legs again. I look down there, thinking he's going to touch me, but he simply holds out a big hand. "Give me your leg."

I lift my leg and place it in his calloused hand, and a strange sensation buzzes in my skin as he wraps his warm fingers around my shin and gently places it in the stirrup.

He's about to grab the leather strap but hesitates, glancing at me and drawing his hand back. "Keep your leg there." He points at the other stirrup. "Put your other leg up."

Swallowing hard, I lift my other leg and place it in the cold metal.

Dax looks back and forth between my unbound legs and my face, and I barely breathe as I wait for his next move.

He steps back around the table and takes my chin in his hand, looking down at me while asking Mikhail, "Is she submissive at heart this one?"

"She is," Mikhail confirms.

Something in Dax's expression changes, something almost soft flickering in his gaze as he absently strokes my cheek with his thumb. "Such a rare thing." Lifting his eyes to Mikhail, he says, "Lucky bastard to train this one." Then his attention is back on me, studying me with something near reverence. It settles something deep within me, holding me in a trance—under his will.

Lifting two fingers to my mouth, he says, "Open up." Instead of the usual bite of his command, there's a gentleness to his tone that has me opening automatically.

He slides his fingers onto my tongue, holding my eyes captive as he strokes. The gesture is oddly intimate, and I find my breathing deepening as I let him invade the personal space and take control over my body.

Slowly, he glides his fingers back out, lingering a moment on my lip. "Good girl."

Something warm and calm washes over me at the sound of those two words, and all I want to do is please him just so I can hear them again. I follow him with my eyes as he pulls the table up, takes a seat on his rolling chair between my legs, and puts on gloves. A special kind of calmness seems to have descended over him as he goes slower than usual, like he's soaking up each moment.

Resting a gloved hand on my inner thigh, he looks at me with insistent yet patient eyes. "Are you gonna be a good girl and let me clean out your bowels?"

I lick my lips and say in a breathy voice, "Yes, Sir."

A smile tips up the corners of his lips, and his praise is even sweeter this time as he says, "Good girl."

When he turns to the tray beside him, I realize I'm breathing deep and loud, through my mouth, all the way into my stomach. And when he lifts the large syringe, smears lube on the tip, and presses it into my narrow hole, I just stare at him.

It's not until water seeps into my belly, unnatural and unwanted, that I react.

A tiny mewl slips past my lips, and I snap my eyes shut, flexing my hands as I tug at the straps. The water keeps coming in a constant flow, and a slow sense of panic creeps along the edges of my mind. I writhe my hips on the surface, wanting to get away from the intrusion.

"Lie still," Dax urges with enough firmness to incite my instant obedience. But alarm keeps building in my body, and my legs twitch in the stirrups as the need to rip them out and close them wars with the need to obey.

Finally, the syringe disappears, and the water settles deep in my belly, where it's less obtrusive.

A warm hand on my stomach has me opening my eyes to look straight into Dax's sincere ones.

"Would you feel better if I tied you down?"

"I—I don't..." the idea soothes the turmoil rolling inside me, but I can't admit it.

"I can see it on your legs," he nods to the side where my leg is still twitching. "You're struggling with yourself. Not having a choice would make it easier."

I give a shake of my head, not getting how he reads it so easily.

"I don't mind." He closes the strap around my ankle and pulls to let me feel the rush of being trapped and helpless. "You've proven your submission plenty."

He proceeds to close every other strap on the table, stroking my skin and holding my gaze as he goes. When he's done, there's not a single thought in my head. There's just him, his calm power, and the irrational peace of being trapped.

My eyelids flutter, wanting to fall shut as a pleasant dizziness fills my head.

I've never felt anything like it, and I find myself never wanting to leave this chair.

I register Dax returning to sit on the stool between my legs just before I let my eyes fall shut, closing me into a peaceful darkness where barely the feeling of the plastic tip sinking into my ass disturbs me.

But once again, I can't ignore the water when Dax pushes more into my belly. Humiliation hovers at the edges of my mind, trying to break through the quiet darkness and infect my thoughts. But when the restlessness tries to take hold of my body, I meet the resistance of the straps. They keep me down like a tight, comforting blanket, stabilizing me through the humiliation.

"Good girl," Dax croons, and when he starts on the next syringe, something odd happens.

The water distends my belly painfully, but the pain mixes with the loss of control—the dominance that competent hands exert over me—and it morphs into something else.

A pulsing heat close to my core.

A moan sounds somewhere in the room, and the moment I realize it's mine, my eyes dart open, staring into gentle eyes that reflect a steadiness strong enough to level me through the storm.

"Close your eyes," Dax gently says, and I do. "Your body knows that it belongs to me right now. Let your mind accept it too."

A voice in the back of my head tells me that it belongs to someone else. Someone far away who laid claim to it before I got here. But the thought quickly drowns in the overwhelming sensation of the water pressing against my belly from the inside.

I moan again, and when Dax begins on the fourth round of water, tears trickle from my eyes. But it's not tears of grief. It's pure overstimulation—pure loss of control—that needs an outlet.

"It's too... too much," I whimper somewhere along the way, my words slurred and weak. I open my eyes only to have them fall shut a moment later, too heavy to keep open. "Too much."

"We're done in a moment."

The pressure builds a little longer, and then the syringe disappears. But the discomfort doesn't fade. It keeps throbbing inside me, needing to get out, and it takes all my drowsy energy to keep it inside.

Someone starts loosening the straps, working quickly, and then I'm hoisted up into strong arms. Long hair tickles my nose as Dax cradles me against his hard chest and carries me through the room to place me on the toilet.

"Are... I..." I try to say something, but can't form the words.

"Let go," a warm voice says as a wide hand cradles the back of my head, tugging me forward to lean against a stomach.

From there on, I barely realize what happens. It's like I'm drugged all over again.

Somewhere along the way, I recognize that it's a

good thing, not being cognizant during the humiliation my body endures. But I also think that it doesn't matter, because there's nothing humiliating about the way large hands gently handle me, carefully washing me and curling me up in a warm lap.

"That was quite fascinating," someone says, and I blink my heavy lids to find Mikhail in a chair across the room, watching with curious eyes. I had completely forgotten he was here.

"She went deep into subspace," Dax says, ruffling my hair gently. "Never seen that happen to a girl in this place before."

"Maybe we should train more women like this. Good money if we find the right buyer, I think."

"I'll definitely be up for it," Dax says. "It gets tiresome with all the screaming sometimes. I swear, some days, I just want to cut all of their vocal cords."

I squirm on his lap as the horror scenario plays out in my head.

"No worries, pretty girl. Not yours," Dax reassures, hugging me tight.

I blink to see Mikhail rub his scruff and cock his head. "I do like them screaming, but the whole brain-twisting part is a good challenge." He taps the side of his head. "Keeps me sharp."

"I wouldn't mind you sending this one my way again."

"Of course. But I'll keep my eye out for submissive tendencies in other girls. Fear tends to cover it up, so we might not see even if it's there."

The two men keep chatting for a while. Disturbing

though the subject might be, I manage to shut it out and rest my head on Dax's shoulder, enjoying the way his fingertips move against my scalp.

He feels strong and steady, and as long as I keep my eyes closed and ignore the voices, I can almost pretend that it's Nikolai holding me, and I drift back into that warm, fuzzy place.

I'm not the same after the chair and the odd episode with Dax.

I still fight Mikhail sometimes when he comes to use me and train my ass, but it's mostly because he provokes me, telling me to tug at my chains or to try to get free when he holds me down. When he doesn't provoke me, I simply go along, pushing up on all fours to display my ass for him, opening my mouth wide when he wants to train my gag reflex, or crawling down the hall in front of him when he's taking me to Dax.

Something must have snapped in my mind. Or maybe settled. It's like knowing how futile escape is has freed up room to accept the situation.

I feel an odd sort of peace, knowing it's all out of my hands. I can't change a thing no matter what I do, so I might as well stop trying.

But that doesn't mean hope is gone.

I still dream about Nikolai, letting my mind take me to him when I lie on the mattress, hugging the teddy close in my chained arms.

I fantasize about him bringing a small army out here to storm the place and free me. But when I imagine them shooting up the place and the men in here—Mikhail and Dax lying dead on the cold stone floor—I'm back in a nightmare, gasping for air.

I know it's bad. I'm developing feelings for my captors. Stockholm syndrome. So I think extra hard about Nikolai to block it out, imagining him stealing down the halls at night, quietly breaking open my cell and carrying me out of here.

It's a wild dream. He may have the resources to search for me and maybe even succeed, but why would he go to such lengths for a girl he has just met? He might not even realize something bad has happened. Most likely, he thinks I changed my mind and bolted.

This is what my logical brain tells me, but something in my gut keeps the dream vivid in my mind. The way he said *mine* when we said goodbye held a promise so deep and sincere I can't let it go. I'm not sure exactly what the promise entailed, but it was a promise of so much more to come.

So I keep him alive in my mind, and when Mikhail brings me back to the chair one day, I close my eyes and imagine it's Nikolai's voice ordering me into it.

I willingly get up, even knowing what torture I'm facing. But when I imagine Nikolai's hands strapping me down, it's like an erotic dream. Dax doesn't need a drop of lube when he comes to insert the dildo.

"She's already dripping," he says, flicking his fingers through my folds.

He has left my ears free today, though the hood is in place over my head, covering my world in darkness.

Steps click over concrete as Mikhail approaches, and I feel his authoritative presence beside me before he slips a finger through my wet lips.

"Dirty girl." He tuts and shoves two fingers inside me, making me gasp. "Such a good little *shlyukha*," he half mocks, half praises. "It's a shame we already have a contract on this one. We could get really good money for her." He draws his fingers back and slams three long ones inside, and I buck against the restraints as pain and pleasure coalesce around the intrusion. "Or I could keep her to myself."

He pumps in and out, drawing out my lust in no time, making me spasm and jerk against the leather straps.

"That's right," Mikhail says. "Struggle all you want. Feel how helpless you are."

I moan at his words. I'm a bit shocked at how easily my brain shuts off these days, but I don't linger on it. There's no use berating myself. It would only bring me more misery. And with the hood over my head, it's easy to pretend this is all a dream.

So I keep bucking, finding comfort in the unforgiving restraints. They free me from my mind with the knowledge that I'm powerless. Nothing I do will get me out of this predicament. The only thing I can do is let go. So I do just that. I let my moans flow free as I give in to the pulsing pleasure thrumming at my core.

"Pl—please, Sir," I stammer through the staggering need. "Can I come?"

"Not until I say so," he growls, and I expect him to pull out, but instead he picks up speed.

I strain my fingers against the wood and curl my toes as an orgasm threatens to rip through my body. "I can't stop it."

"Don't you dare," Mikhail snarls, and I can almost see the cruel sneer on his lips. And God, it drives my need even higher. But somehow, I manage to hold it in, tightening my muscles at my core to keep the sensations from exploding.

The energy swirls in my body, quicker and quicker, spinning my head and driving me insane.

"Please," I beg again, but the answer remains the same.

"No."

"Argh." I strain into the straps, my entire body convulsing as he keeps finger-fucking me with unmerciful speed. I have no idea how I'm not coming. It takes everything I have to hold the orgasm back, and the next few minutes feel like the longest of my life.

"Come!" Mikhail suddenly barks, and it's like a spark to a pool of gasoline. The orgasm explodes at my core, shooting heat waves through my entire body, making me spasm and jerk with a force that has the straps digging deep into my skin. But I barely notice. All I feel is the painful pleasure that rips through me with the force of a high-caliber gun, tearing apart everything in its path.

When Mikhail removes his fingers and steps aside, I slump against the straps, panting hard and spasming every now and then when an aftershock rips through me.

"Do you want me to begin?" Dax asks.

"Go ahead," Mikhail replies.

"What? No? What?" I stutter on bated breaths. I'm not sure what I thought, but as my brain kicks in, I remember what happened in this chair the last time, and my muscles tense with fear. I'm already exhausted. "I can't take anymore."

Mikhail brushes his knuckles over my arm, and his voice is laced with amusement as he says, "I'm afraid you don't have much of a choice, *Koshechka*. But you're welcome to try if you'd like."

"No, no, no." I jerk with each staggered protest, and defeat is like a blow to the gut as I barely move an inch. All I manage is a little wriggling and some flapping of my hands. My voice rises to a high pitch as Dax smears lube onto my pussy and positions the dildo, pushing the tip inside me. "Please..." I whimper, not knowing what to beg for. I know nothing I say will make him stop, and I also know I can't take one more round of sexual torture, shut inside the darkness, alone with my screams and the constant painful pulsing in my body. Something inside me will break for good. "Please... will you just stay? Just stay with me," I say as I remember the cold loneliness with a clarity that bites into my fragile mind. Dax positions the vibrator against my clit, and I add a desperate, "Please, Sir."

Mikhail hums and strokes his hand over my chest and across my collarbone. "Sure, *Koshechka*. Since you ask so sweetly. This is not a punishment. And I want to be here and oversee the training myself."

"Thank—" A yelp breaks off my words as the dildo starts moving, slowly pushing into me. "Thank you, Sir."

"Ah!" I cry out as the vibrator comes alive against my clit. I thought the first orgasm had sated me more than plenty, but suddenly, my core is humming again, pleasure coiling tight within me and sending me toward the edge with frightening speed.

"Good girl. So horny. So ready to take." Mikhail places a finger on each of my nipples and draws circles with a light touch. "Would you like to come again?"

"Yes, please. Yes, Sir," I pant as his touch sends shivers through me, adding to the swirling heat at my core.

He pinches my nipples lightly, making me moan from an erotic twinge of pain. I sense Dax hovering right beside me, and feeling the presence of both men is a relief unlike anything. And Mikhail adds to my relief as he says, "You may come."

A long moan seeps from my mouth as I give in to the vibrations on my clit, clenching my inner walls around the dildo that keeps moving, in and out. The pace is slow, but my body is strummed so tight that I slip straight onto the edge. But just as I press into the vibrator, about to fall over, Mikhail removes his hands, and something snaps onto my nipples, biting hard and deep into my sensitive nubs.

A raw wail rips from my throat, and I squeeze my eyes shut as agony eradicates the pleasure. The orgasm breaks off just as it had started rolling, and I break into tears as the pulsing at my core turns painful and the clamps on my nipples keep squeezing, sending constant jolts through my body. I jerk and twitch against the restraints, but this time for a whole different reason.

"Shh, *Koshechka*," Mikhail soothes, stroking my stomach gently. "Take the pain for me."

Biting my lips, I shake my head against the straps. "I can't."

"Oh yes, you can. I know you want to please me."

I want to deny it, but I can't. And as the pain transforms into waves of heat, it stirs my submission. It might often be hidden beneath layers of shame and learned dos and don'ts, but I do want to please. I crave it. And not just Nikolai who took my submission with consent. I want to please these brutal men too, who have taken my life and everything I was and made me into this helpless, needy creature. So I part my lips and let out the truth. "Yes. I do. I do want to please you."

"Good girl." Mikhail awards me with gentle strokes on my stomach. His light touch raises goosebumps on my sensitive skin, and I start moaning again as pleasure builds anew. "You may come," Mikhail says.

"Thank you, Sir," I pant as I steer straight for the precipice. "Thank you. So much."

An orgasm brews at my core, just about to explode when Mikhail tells Dax, "Take off the clamps."

The words do nothing to reduce the building tension, but what has it shattering once more is when Dax removes the clamps and blood flows back into my sore nipples, giving rise to a whole new wave of throbbing pain.

"No!" I scream as my orgasm once again crashes and my mind threatens to give in under the pressure of it all.

"Oh, yes. We're gonna keep going like this until you come despite the pain. You're gonna be such a good *shlyukha* that can come on command no matter what happens."

"I can't." I try to shake my head against the straps as defeat chokes me up. "I just can't."

"Don't worry, *Koshechka*. I'll help you get there."

"No, it won't work." I yelp as the vibrations intensify, and the pulsing heat coils tight once again. "I can't!" I scream as frustration blots out everything else, knowing they're going to take this orgasm too.

"Yes, you can. I promise I'll get you there," Mikhail says. "Now be a good girl and take that orgasm you so badly want."

"No!" I scream, but the sound morphs into a moan as the dildo speeds up, fucking me quickly and deeply. I strain so hard against the straps that they dig into my skin as I spasm with an onsetting orgasm, but once again, Dax kills it with the clamps.

I scream through the bag as pain, frustration, hot need, and anger coalesce inside me. The vibrations and the dildo slow down, yet I keep screaming. It's all I can do to get the emotions out. Being strapped down tight, I can't even put up a physical fight. So I keep screaming, coughing in between as my throat becomes raw.

They go two more times, intensifying the vibrations, shoving me onto the edge, and killing my orgasm with the clamps. I grow more desensitized to the pain as the pleasure keeps pulsing within me, but they seem to adjust the tightness of the clamps, and it hurts like hell every time they put them on or take them off.

"Stop!" I yell as one of them pulls at the clamps, sending stabs of pain through my overly sensitive nipples. "I fucking hate you! Both of you!"

I vaguely notice something swish through the air just before a hand connects with my cheek and Mikhail's voice booms into the room. "That's no way to talk."

The shock reverberates through me and sends tears to my eyes. Pulling against the wrist straps, I want to lift a hand and cover my burning cheek, but all I can do is sit there and take it. The hopelessness of it all sears deep inside me, and a sob wrenches from my throat, sending me into full-on crying.

"Stop, please stop," I whimper between sniffles, my chest shaking against the straps. "I can't take anymore."

I flinch as Mikhail presses a hand to my cheek. But this time, it's gentle. "Do you want to be a good girl, *Koshechka?*"

"Y—yes," I stutter. "I do."

"Then give me my orgasm."

"I can't." Hopelessness gnaws through me, and a deep sob wrenches from my gut. "I just can't."

"Why not?"

"The pain."

"The pain *I'm* giving you," Mikhail says. "And you want to please me, don't you?"

"Yes." And his gentleness makes me want to do so even more. I want to lean into his tender hand, and I want the bag gone to feel his skin against mine. But I can't have either. All I have are his softly spoken words, so I soak them up and let them soothe me.

"Then accept the pain and let it drive you instead of stopping you."

I swallow back a protest. Because I know he's right.

I'm still fighting, and as long as I am, I won't be able to come.

He curves both hands around my cheeks and leans so close I can feel his breath through the material covering my head. "I want you to ask me for an orgasm really nicely, and if you don't deliver this time, you're gonna ask me for a punishment, and you won't get to come today."

The closeness and the soft, yet steady command in his voice work like a drug on my mind. My crying fades to silent shakes in my chest, and the tears stop flowing as he draws me into that fluffy space, where all I want to do is obey.

"Do you hear me?" he adds when I don't answer, rubbing my skin through the coarse material.

I wet my dry lips. "Yes. I understand."

"Good. Now ask me."

"Sir"—I steady myself with a shuddery inhale—"can I come for you?"

He gives a warm chuckle, probably because of the last two words I added myself. "Yes, my sweet *shlyukha*. Come for me."

The vibrations intensify again, and the dildo moves both faster and deeper, sending staggering bursts of painful pleasure deep into my core. "Ah," I cry, bucking into the restraints.

"Can you feel it?" Mikhail mocks right in front of me, still cupping my face. "That you're trapped? You have no choice. No way of escape."

"Yes," I moan, bucking into the straps again to feel

the sweet resistance. I shut off my mind as I give in to everything. His devastating control, my utter helplessness, and the staggering sensations in my body. I go limp against the chair, letting my body react however it needs, shuddering as pleasure rips through me, sending long moans up from deep within my belly.

"That's it. You're nothing but a sweet little whore here to give me what I want. Accept it and obey."

Mikhail's words spur me on.

"And in a moment, Dax will rip the clamps off, and it's gonna hurt *so* fucking bad."

"No, no, no," I whimper, but this time, the fear does nothing to hinder the pleasure. Rather, it seeps into me as a pulsing energy, driving my need until I'm panting hard with an onsetting orgasm.

Hands grab onto the clamps, pulling slightly, but this time, I let the pain drive me. Like the fear, it becomes fuel to the fire burning within me.

"Yes," I moan, and when Dax pulls a little harder, I repeat a little louder. "Yes."

"Come!" Mikhail demands, and the rumbling force of his voice sets my orgasm rolling with a staggering intensity that has me spasming and jerking so hard my feet cramp.

Dax rips off the clamps, sending searing pain unlike any of the previous times bursting through my nerves. It clashes with the pleasure in a violent explosion, and I scream as the orgasm tears through me like a too-strong electrical current that threatens to burn down the whole system.

It keeps rolling, on and on. Dax twists my abused nipples, but this time there's no pain. It's liquid fire that keeps me shuddering and jerking as mind-numbing pleasure takes over my world until I can't see anymore.

The electric current fades, and finally, I crash. Into blissful darkness.

CHAPTER
10

The days blur together. I have no idea how long I've been here—if the two months are coming to an end, or if I still have weeks to go. But as things slowly change, I begin to sense the end closing in. It begins with more time in the workout room and Dorin drilling me to practice cardio and strengthen my muscles—especially my legs. Then my time spent in the chair escalates as Mikhail ramps up the training to make me into the perfect little slut that can come on command, hold back orgasms under intense stimulation or get them despite severe pain, then take a cock deep into my throat and give a good blow job even though I'm about to pass out from exhaustion.

I ask Mikhail how much time I have left here, but he won't grant me an answer. I'm not sure I really want one. I'm not sure I want to know anything about my impending life outside these walls. Yet I can't help probing.

"Who is he? The man who has bought me," I ask one morning when Mikhail waits for me to finish my breakfast.

"You'll find out soon enough."

"What is he going to do to me?"

Mikhail smirks. "That's up to him."

"Is he going to hurt me?" I clutch the bowl between my hands.

"Depends on what you mean. By your definition, I'm sure he will. But compared to what most girls here experience, I don't think so."

I gulp. "What happens to the other girls?"

"Sold to the highest bidder, usually on auction, and then we'll train them to their liking. A special training regiment is expensive, though, so some buyers choose a girl from final auction—that's for girls who have finished their training."

"And how does he want me?"

Mikhail smirks. "Pliant and obedient. Ready to please. A good little *shlyukha,* who can come on command, handle pain, and give good head."

I gulp, and the movement makes my tongue piercing click against my teeth. I still have no idea what it's for. A few days ago, Dax told me it has fully healed and I don't need the mittens anymore, but he wouldn't tell me what the piercing is for. They don't even chain my arms anymore, arrogantly confident that I won't disobey and touch my pussy without permission. And even though I sometimes consider doing it anyway to retain some kind of autonomy, I can't. I'm not sure if it's the threat to repeat my first devastating, lonely time in the chair that holds me back or if it's because the mere thought of disobeying has my stomach all twisted up in knots.

"Is he the one who wanted the piercing?" I ask,

hoping Mikhail will grant me some answers.

"Indeed."

"Why?"

"You'll see soon enough."

Clenching my molars, I look off to the side. Once the worst of the frustration settles, I return my attention to Mikhail and change my direction of questioning. "What happens to the girls who don't get sold?"

"Dorin takes care of them."

My eyes must grow wide as teacups as I consider what that means. "How?" I don't want to know, but I can't not ask.

"Dorin might seem like a brute, but he's really quite merciful in his way of getting rid of girls." Mikhail sinks to his haunches in front of me and wraps a hand around my throat. "Do you remember how I made you faint on the train?" He moves his fingers a bit as if searching for something, then presses into the sides of my neck. "If I block the oxygen supply to your brain—closing off your veins—you'll lose consciousness."

A dizzy sensation begins to drag me down, making my body feel heavy.

"Then he snaps their neck." A sharp sound makes me jump as he snaps his fingers. He releases me, and the fog clears, although slowly. "They don't feel a thing. Well, at least not physically. They usually know what's coming when he takes them away."

My pulse pounds so hard that a wave of nausea rises at the back of my throat, and I set the bowl aside to press my head into my hands.

"Don't worry, *Koshechka*." He moves onto the

mattress and lifts me into his lap. "I told you. You're special. That won't happen to you."

"What if he decides he doesn't want me anyway?" I burrow into his shoulder, so used to the contradictory coexistence of his cruelty and tenderness by now that I easily seek his comfort.

"He won't."

"How do you know?"

"I know him. And he keeps calling me, wanting updates. It's bloody annoying. I keep telling him to let me do my job, but he won't let up."

I breathe a bit calmer at hearing this. I probably shouldn't, though. This man just might want me for all the wrong reasons, and obsession can be a dangerous thing. But these days, I find comfort where I can—rational or irrational.

"Now, get on all fours so I can get your ass ready for your master." Mikhail retrieves a butt plug a size bigger than the one he used on me yesterday from his pocket. He has been doing this every day after breakfast for a while now, shoving a plug inside my ass and making me wear it until he brings me the next meal. They slowly get bigger, and I'm achingly aware of where this is going to end.

But I don't want to think about it, and as I get on all fours and succumb to Mikhail's devastating will, it's easy to forget. I shut off my brain and all the thoughts of my new master, the piercing, and the girls that Dorin *gets rid of.*

But once Mikhail has fucked me into oblivion with the plug seated deep inside me, fed me kasha, and held me until I stop shuddering and shaking and leaves me alone, it all filters back in.

It takes me days of nightmares and crawling anxiety to get the image of Dorin snapping a girl's neck out of my mind, and I can't stop wondering and worrying what my master will do to me. So I don't ask more questions about him or this place. Instead, I start fantasizing about Nikolai again. Sometimes, the thoughts are so vivid that I fear I'm going mad. But worrying about things that actually will happen might just do the same. And I'd rather that my insanity be full of hopefulness than misery.

As I immerse myself in hopeful fantasies of fairytale-like rescues and Nikolai sweeping me away into kinky realms that are scarily similar to the one I'm stuck in, I grow convinced that I'm losing my mind.

My fantasies about Nikolai escalate to a point where they are so vivid I can barely tell reality from dream anymore. Mikhail may say he's not supposed to break me, but I think he has actually done it.

When I'm in the chair, bound and blindfolded, I can almost sense Nikolai. I keep catching these small drifts of his fresh, earthy scent, thinking he's there. But another inhale only fills my nose with the scent of dry basement. Then I think I feel his hands on my body, smooth and strong, stroking my skin and grabbing my throat. But every time the hood comes off, it's Mikhail's long fingers on my skin, freeing the straps and carrying me back to my cell, where he holds me until the shaking settles and I fall asleep.

One day, the feeling becomes so strong I can't

contain it.

"Nikolai?" I say as smooth hands run over my body, driving me insane with the mix of pleasure and pain that I first came to know as Nikolai's special brand of affection. But now the combination has become tainted by the cruelty of this place.

"Nikolai," I repeat as fingers tweak a nipple while a hand gently strokes my thighs.

Still no response.

"Please, just tell me if it's you," I beg as tears leak from my eyes. "I can't take this anymore. Please, just talk to me."

"Quiet," Mikhail demands.

But I keep sensing the scent of pine trees—feeling his strong presence hovering above me.

One week with Nikolai has branded the juxtaposition of quiet calm and demanding authority so deep into me that I can conjure the sensation with vivid precision.

My mind knows it isn't real, but my body can't feel it. So I keep pressing, tears trickling down my cheeks and wetting the fabric as I jostle in the restraints. "Please," I beg as panicked urgency builds inside me. "Just one word. I need to know it's you."

The dildo stops buzzing inside me, and two strong hands curve around my shoulders, thumbs stroking back and forth along my sensitive skin.

"Nikolai, is that you?" I say, and when I don't get an answer, the insanity breaks loose.

I scream at the top of my lungs, jerking against the restraints so the leather digs into my skin. If my head

138

wasn't strapped in so tightly, I'd be banging it against the wood. But not even the choice to hurt myself is mine. So I keep screaming and jerking, hurting my throat and chafing my skin.

Long fingers wrap around my neck, flexing at the sides. Mikhail squeezes, shutting off the blood flow and dulling my senses.

I think the strong hands on my shoulders are still there, trying to calm me. But they can't be. They're not calloused enough to belong to Dax or Dorin, and Mikhail's fingers are on my throat, draining the strength from my body, shutting off my system.

My mind blurs, and I sag in the chair as someone works on the straps.

I'm barely cognizant when someone hoists me up—the hood still over my head—nestling me against a strong chest as he carries me back to my cell, places me on the mattress, and chains me to the wall. Then I'm pulled into a strong chest, being rocked with a gentleness that hurts my hollowed-out mind.

The scent of pine trees keeps pervading my senses, and I cry like a child, for everything I've lost, everything I've endured, and all the things I won't regain. The loss of the man, my mind, and my free will.

CHAPTER
11

"Put these on," Mikhail says one night, throwing a stack of clothes on the mattress. "And these." A pair of sneakers thud against the floor as he drops them in front of me.

I stare at the items, unable to comprehend what's going on.

"Let's go." He claps his hands, spurring me into action.

I grab the red blouse on top of the pile and push my arms through the sleeves. The fabric feels strange against my skin. Wrong.

"Where am I going?" I ask as I stick my head through the blouse, but Mikhail is on his way out, leaving me with a ton of questions as the door falls shut with a heavy clank.

Anxiety roils in my belly as I proceed to put on panties and jeans, followed by socks and shoes.

Then I wait.

I haven't seen a clock for ages and have no idea what a minute feels like anymore, but I can almost hear the time ticking, the minutes passing at a dreadfully slow pace.

When the door opens again, I'm fidgeting, pinching the edge of the mattress, twisting my fingers, and tugging at the hem of the blouse.

"What's going on?" I ask Mikhail.

"It's your lucky day." He steps back into the hall, and I know I'm supposed to follow since he leaves the door ajar.

I rush after him, struggling to keep up with his long strides. "Am I going somewhere?" I ask in a thin voice. "Is he here?"

My stomach twists. I've somehow gotten so used to the fucked-up depravity of this place, maybe even gotten comfortable with the routines, that the thought of leaving makes me sick with worry.

What if the next place is even worse? What if this man who has bought me is a sadistic psychopath wanting to hurt me for the fun of it? What if he locks me up and forgets to feed me? Simply lets me wither away?

Mikhail leads me down several long halls before he stops at a metal door even heavier than the one to my cell. He presses his finger to the biometric scanner on the wall and shoves the door wide open.

My heart skips a beat as I see what's on the other side. A long flight of concrete stairs leads right into the open. Tall trees and a starry night sky. Fresh air and the scent of pine trees and moss.

Closing my eyes, I inhale deeply. The fresh air fills my senses with a surge of hope. I feel like I can almost touch it, the freedom. So close.

"You have one chance to get away," Mikhail says,

making me snap back to the present—the dry air and the dusty smell of basement. "If you manage, you're free."

I stare at him, through the door, and back up at him, suddenly struck by a wistful feeling.

Despite everything he has done, I've come to care for him. Or maybe grown attached because he's the only thing I have to cling to down here—the only thing keeping me from drowning. Or breaking, as he'd say.

But am I not broken?

I've accepted his will and succumbed to his degradations. I've let him strip me of all dignity and reduce me to this pliant person I hardly recognize. He has driven me so far out I'm seeing things that aren't even there.

Yet the thought of never feeling his arms around me again has my heart aching.

But just like his comfort, this wistfulness is false. It's Stockholm syndrome. Survival.

So I squeeze my eyes shut and conjure images of the man who actually cared about me—whose touch was filled with genuine sympathy and affection.

If I have any chance at getting back to him—even with the very real possibility of him having forgotten about me—I need to grab onto it and fight with everything I have.

So I give a firm nod. "Okay."

I have no idea where I am, where this forest leads, or if I'll die trying. It doesn't matter. This is my only chance.

"You have a fifteen-minute head start." Mikhail takes out a stopwatch and presses the top.

I stare at him for a moment. Is this it? No goodbye,

no last words. I actually thought he cared about me—on some level. But the tender strokes across my forehead and the tight embraces when I cried were all just a means to an end. A method of quickly and effectively bending me to his will.

The realization is like a splash of cold water, ripping me out of the illusion with cruel force.

"Better make them count," Mikhail says, and I shove down the urge to run into his arms for one final hug and set off up the stairs.

* * *

Adrenaline pulses through my veins, my legs pounding from the strain of my speed. I nearly trip over branches and stones several times, but somehow, I manage to keep upright, the wind whirring past my ears as I burst through the trees.

I don't look back. Not once. If I do, I'll only waver, and I can't afford that.

So I run until my lungs burn, and then I run some more.

My nape prickles with awareness as if someone's watching me, and once in a while, I think I hear twigs snag behind me and feel a presence lurking close by.

But I still don't turn. I keep going. Not thinking, not wondering, just running. Deeper and deeper into the thick woods.

Only when I feel like I'm about to collapse from exertion does my rational brain kick in. Knowing I can't keep going like this, I start scouting for places to hide. A tree I can climb, a gathering of large rocks, or a fallen trunk.

With the dense thicket of tree tops only allowing a sliver of the pale moonlight to seep through, I can't see much, so I end up choosing a particularly thick tree as cover. It only hides me from anyone approaching from behind me, so if Mikhail has sent men searching for me from different directions, it won't do me much good. But it's better than trying to climb one of the impossibly tall trunks or trying to merge with the ground.

My breath wheezes in and out of my nose, filling the quiet night with too much sound. I try to breathe through my mouth instead, licking my lips as the air rushes past them, but it doesn't do me much good. The sound is pervasive no matter how I breathe.

When I hear the dull thuds of stealthy footsteps behind me, I slam my hand over my mouth. I stop breathing entirely as my system goes into overdrive, beating with the urge to run. But I can't break my cover.

Not until I feel it. A hand grabbing for my arm.

I shove off the tree, miraculously slipping out of his grip. My feet pound against the soil, but so does another set of much heavier steps. Right behind me.

Hands grab me. Hard. I fly back, slamming into a wide chest. My reaction is instant and instinctive. With a wail that tears through the night, I kick back against long legs and shove at a thick arm that bands around my chest. Corded muscles bulge beneath my fingers as I dig into his skin. His torso feels just as strong as I try to push off him. A wall of muscle rippling against my back.

There's no escaping this man.

I gasp when he whips me around and shoves me against the wide trunk.

Then hands are on my hips, yanking down my pants, ripping the flimsy panties.

I try to turn my head to see who has caught me, but a massive hand pins my head against the trunk. All I see are trees and pale moonlight.

I can't recognize the hands. They're too big to belong to Mikhail, too smooth to belong to Dax or Dorin. Yet they seem achingly familiar. But none of the other guards in the basement has ever touched me.

The hands prod at my opening, and I whimper as they slide through my slick lips. I'm always wet at the hands of brutal men. Mikhail did train me well as he promised. Or I'm just fucked-up.

It doesn't matter. The fingers shove inside, making me buck from the force.

A gentle breeze drifts through the trees, caressing my cheek and bringing me the earthy scent of a cologne with hints of pine.

No, it can't be.

I squeeze my eyes shut and inhale again. It's the exact same scent that became branded deep into my brain when large hands held me down, took my breath, fucked me brutally, and then caressed me sweetly.

It's so real. So painfully real.

There's no fabric covering my head to muddle the scent and induce doubt. And the hands... I suddenly remember with startling clarity. They are his too. *Nikolai.* The man I've dreamed about every day throughout this nightmare. He's here! I'm not insane.

"Is that you?" I whisper, then imbue my voice with more strength. "Niko—"

A large hand cuts off the word as it presses onto my mouth.

"Shh," he lulls, shutting off my airflow with a big palm, fingers pinching my nose.

I don't know what happens. It's not a conscious choice. It's something instinctive and reflexive that shuts me down. The urge to submit or maybe the familiar feeling of safety. Maybe the obedience taught at the terrifyingly competent hands of Mikhail. It doesn't matter.

My body gives in and my brain turns quiet.

"Hmm," he hums as I sink into him, and he lifts his other hand to caress my temple.

It's strangely intimate—the stroking and the choking, the safety and the fear. It goes to my head, pulling me deep into a warm, floaty space.

But the peace doesn't last. It never does.

As the need to breathe intensifies, burning in my lungs, I start twitching. But I still don't fight. Not until instinct takes over. My reactions are out of my control when my hands fly up to grab the hand over my mouth. My captor releases my nose, just long enough to let me draw in air. Then he clamps my airway shut again, leaving my breath wholly under the control of this mighty man.

My hands fall back down, hanging at my sides. I don't even struggle when the sound of a belt and a zipper works its way through my brain, or when fingers flick through my pussy.

It's only when a cock presses against my opening that I snap out of the trance.

Suddenly, I writhe between the trunk and the man. But he simply puts more weight on my back, and I'm left to uselessly flail my hands as he forces his way inside me.

Panic rises, restricting my lungs and dragging whimpers from my throat. But there's also something else. A hot, urgent pounding. The need to arch back and lose myself to strong hands.

He releases my nose, allowing me another breath before he shuts off my airways again.

Helplessness becomes a cloudy veil over my mind as he sinks into me with a slowness that has me feeling every devastating inch of the intrusion. I don't control anything. Not my breath, not my body, and not even the throbbing need gathering at my core. I grapple at the bark, seeking purchase through the overwhelming mix of sensations. It's all I can do.

"Mine," he growls against my ear, sending a flurry of shivers and butterflies through my system as I recognize the possessive rumble.

Tears spring to my eyes, a moan rising in my throat.

I can't tell if I want this anymore; I can't tell if it really is him. My mind is wrought with the need to find out, but it's no use. So I give up. I give in to the cloudy haze and let primal desire take my body.

A deep groan rumbles in his chest as he senses the moment I give in. He goes still, pausing with the head of his cock just inside my opening. And then he slams inside. So hard I dig my nails into the tree as I buck back.

I cry out, but the sound dies in his hand.

"Don't say a fucking word." He releases my mouth, and the forest fills with my screams and moans—the sound of flesh slapping against flesh. He keeps pounding, sending shock waves through my core, into my body, making me spasm and writhe.

"Don't come," he growls and bites into my neck, awakening new waves of sensation. Pain mixing with pleasure. Pleasure mixing with pain.

Pulling out, he throws me to the ground, stomach-down. Flashes of brown boots and green hunting pants flicker in my vision. A rifle tossed aside on the ground. Then something wet runs down between my ass cheeks. Spit, I realize at another *pfft* sound.

The only protest I manage is a long, plaintive moan as he drags his cock through the moisture and positions himself against my narrow opening. My breath comes in heavy pants as he starts pressing. I shake my head against the ground. *He's too big.* It doesn't matter how well Mikhail has trained me; there's no way I'm taking this man without tearing. But my ass isn't all Mikhail has trained. Even as my mind is reeling from flashes of panic, I can't protest. Because deep down, I want this. I want to be taken by force—taken by competent hands and have my body reduced to an object.

And most of all, I want this: unmerciful, unrelenting possession. I want to be *owned.*

Something happens as he wraps his strong hand around my nape, pinning me to the ground as he starts the slow process of pushing inside me. My brain tells me to fight, but something familiar and safe tugs at me, blending with the submission that has become second nature at the terrifyingly competent hands of Mikhail. I don't *want* to fight. I want to give in. Feel the sweet peace of giving up myself to another person.

So I do just that. I slump as I let go, slackening my muscles and allowing him to advance. I pant hard as he presses past my tight ring of muscle. His wide size burns against my narrow walls, but the pain mixes with a crackling sensation as all my sensitive nerves down there spark to life.

I tremble beneath him as he sinks deeper into me, every inch a testament to his power and my surrender.

His growl reverberates through the night, a primal declaration of conquest—the hunter having caught his prey. Leaning over me, he traps me beneath his weight as he starts fucking me, hard and unrelenting. I cling to the earth, digging my fingers into the soil to seek purchase through the violent storm that threatens to tear my world apart, or maybe mend it.

I don't know; I can't see anything through the storm of his possession. It wraps around my mind, blurs my world, and coils at my core with licks of fire circling each other, faster and faster, into a whirlwind about to explode.

He grows impossibly hard inside me, and I squeeze my eyes shut as my sensitive tissues burn around him. But the pain does nothing to hinder the blast of desire. If anything, it adds to it.

"Come," he demands, just as he shoots his cum inside me, marking me in the most primal of ways. I crash over the edge, screaming into the night as I buck into him.

Resting his weight on his elbows on each side of my face, he leans down and pebbles tiny kisses across my neck. Shivers scurry down my arms, and I crane my neck to allow him better access. I want to stay here forever, safely nestled into the shield of his strong body.

But when he withdraws and I lose his warmth, it's like an icy gust of wind, shuddering through my bones and sending painful clarity to my mind.

I have no idea who this man is. He's not Nikolai. I'm only imagining things. And if I don't get away, I will get sold off to a stranger. Maybe this one, maybe someone else. I have no idea, and I can't take that chance. So I stagger to my feet, glancing behind me to see the back of a tall, broad figure as he pulls something out of a bag. Maybe a blanket. I don't know; I don't care. This is my final shot, so I take it.

I bolt forward, struggling to make my heavy limbs comply and shaking from the last ripples of the orgasm.

Heavy steps pound behind me as he gives chase, and I whimper as I put in all my strength, my lungs burning with exertion. I keep going even knowing I don't stand a chance in living hell. He's right behind me. At any moment, he'll snatch me and throw me to the ground.

But it doesn't happen.

I whip my head back when I realize the thuds of his steps are gone. And he's gone too. All I see are trees. I keep going, almost slamming into trunks as I whip my head from side to side, expecting him to jump me from the side.

My energy quickly fades, and fear becomes a vise

around my chest, keeping my breaths shallow and painful even as I slow down. I stop to catch my breath. I have to, or I'll collapse and become a sitting duck.

Pressing my sweaty palms to my knees, I lean forward, panting. Movement at the edges of my vision makes me look up. I'm about to set off again when something moves between the trees. But then I see the swish of a fluffy tail. Something red. A white tip.

I freeze as I gaze into the low bushes. The moon casts its pale light through the treetops, lighting up the small clearing I'm standing in. A slow wind rustles through the forest, and an owl hoots in the distance.

It's peaceful. Quiet.

The red fur moves, and then I see it. A beautiful fox appears between the trees, coming straight toward me.

It sniffs the ground, the black nose twitching as the tail swishes above the moss. Then it looks up and stops as it sees me.

I hold my breath as I stare into the eyes of the beautiful creature. I've always dreamed about seeing a fox in more than flashes of red disappearing into the night. And here it is, on this fateful night.

I usually don't believe in signs, but this must be one. How can it not?

The fox lowers itself to its hind legs, curling the tail around itself as it watches me. I carefully move a hand from my thigh, and it remains. So I move the other as well, wanting to sink to my knees too.

But then I hear it. A twig snapping.

The fox gets up, ears pointing into the air, ready to bolt too.

There's a swish through the air, and I jerk at a sharp sting in my right butt cheek. Time seems to slow down as I blink toward the fox, staggering a step forward as my balance wavers. Turning my head, I see a small dart lodged in my ass.

I stare at the fox as I drop to my knees, my head swimming and the forest blurring before me.

I fall forward, hitting the ground with a thud, and red fur flashes in my peripheral vision as the fox leaps away.

I've lost, is all I can think. They've caught me. I've squandered my only chance at escape.

Pine needles crunch gently as feet move toward me. A pair of brown boots appear, the vision distorted and hazy. Turning my head slightly, I blink to focus my gaze on the man who crouches before me, but all I see is camouflage clothes and something long. A rifle.

Fingers move over my cheek to brush my long hair from my face, and the faint scent of an earthy cologne hits my nose. The hand trails farther down in one long, firm stroke, over my back and down to my ass, where it pulls out the dart.

"Mine," a deep voice says with fierce possession as the man who shot me wraps a hand around my neck.

"Nikolai. Is that..." I close my eyes, the world spinning too quickly before me. "Is that you?" I manage just before the world fades and I slip into a dreamland.

12

The sound of the heavy door in my cell wakes me. I groan as I blink against the artificial lights and see a pair of sleek leather shoes step inside. It takes me a moment to realize they're not the same brown ones with perforations and a round toe that Mikhail wears. These are smooth and black with a square toe. Less flashy, more elegant.

But the realization holds little meaning to me. I just want to rest my weary body and go back to sleep, so I turn my back to whoever is there and hug my teddy tight.

"Time to go home," a smooth baritone says.

The voice doesn't belong to Mikhail either.

It belongs to someone I've been dreaming about since the day they took me—the man I always think about when hugging the teddy.

But it can't be. My mind is playing yet another trick on me, crueler than any of the previous as the hallucination takes on vivid form, more clear and real than ever before.

He sinks to his haunches behind me, and when a big,

smooth hand touches my shoulder, tears slip from my eyes.

I shake my head, feeling utterly broken. I can't take it anymore. I can't keep hoping and imagining. It hurts too much when the illusion fades.

The hand gently pulls at me, turning me onto my back, and when I stare into a familiar face that doesn't belong down here, I shake my head more ardently. "It's not you," I murmur, closing my eyes again.

He leans down, and the scent of pine and wet moss swamps me with such clarity that I break into tears.

"It is me," the voice says softly against my ear. "I've been here all week, and now I'm taking you home."

A hand comes to my cheek, caressing softly. Genuinely. Mikhail's touch is never this genuine. Nothing down here is.

So I allow myself to look again, and this time, I know it's not a dream. The touch, the scent, his voice. His eyes. It really is him.

I stare at him, tears brimming in my eyes, and for the first time down here, I don't want to hide.

We watch each other for several minutes, me baring my soul and all my innermost private emotions to him as he traces the lines of my face and wipes away the tears that roll down my cheeks.

"Why?" I finally ask, needing to know why he had me kidnapped and stuck in hell for two months when I was already like putty in his hands.

Nikolai wraps his hand around my chin and strokes his thumb along my jaw. "I have very specific needs and a busy schedule. Letting you go meant risking you'd get caught in your head. And then it would have been a real hassle to fix the mess."

"Couldn't you just have taken me with you?"

He lifts an incredulous brow. "And risk having you run off while I was busy or go to the police after I had chained you up?"

"Aren't you afraid I'll do that after..." I bite my lip, not knowing what to call it. So I gesture to the space around me. "This."

Nikolai gathers my wrists in one big hand, curling the other around my neck. My breathing instantly deepens as I melt beneath him, staring into his eyes in utter surrender.

A smile curves his lips. "Not really. Mikhail has trained you well."

Hard heels click behind us, and Mikhail's smug voice breaks the moment. "Indeed I have. Though, it wasn't a very hard job with this one."

Without releasing my throat, Nikolai turns to Mikhail. "So, maybe I should demand half my money back?"

Mikhail scoffs. "You should just be grateful that I didn't sell her to someone else for double the price. Or keep her for myself. It was quite tempting."

Nikolai turns back to me, expression crackling with something cold and dark as he spears me with his intense gaze while speaking to Mikhail. "Good thing you refrained, or she would have been the last girl you sold."

Something stirs inside me, beneath the fear and confusion. Something deep and instinctive. I shrink back at the sight of the smoldering cruelty in his eyes even as I lean my neck up into the collar of his hand.

"See what I mean?" Nikolai says, this time talking to me. "You're mine."

I nod against his hand, not grasping what's happening to me, but feeling the full brunt of it as a potent force swooshes through my body and fills every little cell of my being. At this very moment, I know he's right. I won't go to the police no matter what he does to me. He may drag me through another two months of hell. It doesn't matter, as long as he's ultimately the one in control.

I trust him. It's not rational, but rational became a void concept to me long ago. And I don't trust him in a normal sense, but in the only way that counts. I trust him not to break me.

So I draw my chin toward my chest in deep-felt reverence as he releases my neck.

"Is the harness ready?" Nikolai asks.

"Dax will be in with it in a minute," Mikhail replies.

"Let me see your tongue." Nikolai holds two fingers in front of my mouth, grabs my tongue when I open up, and pulls it out to inspect the piercing. "Very pretty. I can't wait to use it."

I don't know what he means and I can't imagine what it might be. How would someone use a tongue piercing? Even after two months, I'm still baffled by the small thing, unable to see how it could serve as another means to put me in my place.

"Close your mouth." Nikolai releases my tongue and pats my cheek.

More steps enter the room, this time heavy thuds of

boots.

Nikolai gets up to see the harness Dax has brought, and I push up to sit on my knees.

"I haven't tried it on yet—figured you should be the one to do it—but I've measured her head, so the fit should be just right," Dax says.

Nikolai sinks to his haunches before me again, and I watch the brown leather straps in his hands that are connected in various places to form some kind of structure I can't quite make out. "You'll look very pretty in this one." He swipes his thumb across my cheek. "Very helpless."

My thighs clench. *All I crave is to be helpless beneath this man.*

He pulls the straps over my head, adjusts a few ones, and buckles them in several places. When he grabs my chin to inspect the result, my head is strapped into a tight net of thin leather straps that go down over my forehead, past each side of my nose, and around each side of my head. They don't restrict anything—I can still see, hear, breathe normally, and open my mouth to speak. But I have a feeling that won't last. The straps close to my mouth and the ones under my chin still hang loose, and I have a feeling it has something to do with the piercing.

Nikolai confirms this when he tells me to stick my tongue out again and removes the top ring on the barbel.

Dax hands him a piece of thick leather with a flat plate about an inch long protruding from the center. The plate feels like metal covered in silicone as Nikolai places it on top of my tongue, sliding the small hole in the middle over the barbel. He attaches the ring on top, trapping my tongue against the plate, and my heart speeds up as the restrictive feeling intrudes upon my senses.

The small plate goes inside my mouth, pushing my tongue with it, as Nikolai presses the leather over my mouth and buckles it in place. A panel gag, I realize. He finishes by buckling the strap under my chin, forcing my mouth closed over the plate.

I try to wriggle my tongue, but the plate presses it down, flattening it at the bottom of my mouth. I can't even move my jaw. The feeling is obtrusive unlike anything else. I've been tied to a chair, head and limbs immobilized as my body was forced to take orgasm after orgasm. Now, my arms and legs are free, yet the feeling of having my head, even my tongue, strapped in place is even more restrictive than the chair.

I whimper as a floaty sort of sensation descends upon my mind. I stare at Nikolai with aching vulnerability, feeling the meager remains of my autonomy rattle to the floor before him. There's no wanting or not wanting this. This is who I am now. *His.* Through and through.

"She should be able to move the sides of her tongue just enough to swallow, so you'll avoid excessive drooling," Dax explains. "But if you want a different effect, I have a ring gag too with a plate for the piercing." He hands Nikolai a small item. "And this one. My personal favorite."

Nikolai's expression lights up as he looks the small thing over. It's similar to the silicone-covered metal plate depressing my tongue, only this one is wider and double.

Two plates meld together at the end to form a sort of U with holes in each plate.

My eyes go round as I realize that my tongue is supposed to go between the two plates.

"For public?" Nikolai asks with a bright smile as he holds the thing up and looks at Dax. "Without the harness?"

"No one will be able to see it," Dax explains. "Of course, she'll be able to open her mouth, but she won't be able to speak."

Nikolai grabs my jaw and aims all his sharp attention at me. "I don't think you'll want to open your mouth when I'm taking you into the public with this thing on your tongue, will you?"

I shake my head, drawing a shuddery breath through my nose as I imagine being among other people with my tongue stuck in the small device, a constant reminder of Nikolai's inescapable ownership.

"Say something," Mikhail orders.

I try, but my words come out as muffled strings of *aaas* and *iiis*, and mortification washes over me, making my head fall forward with the urge to hide. I've taken so many humiliations at the hands of Mikhail and Dax, and even Dorin, but somehow, having my tongue immobilized and my ability to communicate stolen away affects me the most. And maybe even more so because it's in front of the man I've dreamed of—the man I eagerly want to please.

"So pretty," Nikolai says as he lifts my chin and studies the handiwork.

I want to crumble at his feet. The harness has

snuffed out whatever resistance I had left and reduced me to something that's not my own anymore.

But when he wraps a firm hand around my nape and pulls my forehead to his chest, it's not the devastating loss I feel. It's the deep peace of belonging.

"Mine," he says, as if he knows exactly what I'm thinking. And that's it. Like a switch, his word shuts off the rest of the world, wrapping me in a cocoon of floaty submission.

"I suggest you let her use the toilet while we go get the last things," Dax says when Nikolai pulls back and lets me sit up straight again.

Dax and Mikhail leave the cell, closing the door behind them, and Nikolai orders me to use the toilet, standing in front of me with arms crossed over his wide chest as I relieve myself.

A few minutes later, Mikhail and Dax return, carrying a large wooden cargo box long enough to fit a person.

I gulp as I watch them set it down in the middle of the cell.

"On your knees, your back to the room," Dax orders, pointing at the mattress.

I gingerly sink into position, breathing heavily at the sound of metallic rattling as he comes up behind me. He starts by wrapping a wide leather belt around my waist. Reaching his arms around me, he closes the belt on my stomach, making me gasp each time he yanks at one of the two straps to close it. His touch is mechanical and practical like he's preparing a package for send-off. To him, I'm an object without a voice—without the right to an opinion.

And that's exactly how I feel. But instead of tearing at me and tensing my muscles, the thought frees me. There's no need to struggle, consider what I *should* feel, or what they think about me. So I give up all thought and all self, swaying along with Dax's ministrations, pliant in mind and body as he shoves me forward and places me on all fours.

"Spread her ass," Dax says, and Mikhail steps in to spread my cheeks apart while Dax drips cold lube onto my narrow opening and slips the tip of a small dildo inside. He turns it a little and moves the tip in and out a few times, but it's not to tease or titillate. He's simply taking care not to break me in the process. The moment my muscles loosen, he pushes past my sphincter and all the way inside with one smooth motion.

I whimper as my nerves flare alive, and when he spreads my pussy open and presses a wide dildo against my other opening, I start jerking and making small involuntary wriggles as electricity sparks in my overly sensitive folds.

"Be still." Dax smacks my ass, and I dig my fingers into the mattress as he shoves the toy in. He doesn't even need to pry or use lube. I'm so wet and ready that the wide toy slides right in despite the dildo in my ass narrowing the space.

I groan and moan behind the leather as I struggle to rein in the flaring need bursting through my body. The need only grows when Dax pulls a strap between my legs, making me realize that the toys are attached to it as he pulls it tight and the dildos sink deeper into me.

Helplessness becomes an intoxicating drug on my mind as he attaches the strap to the waist belt, locking the toys in place deep inside me.

Tears spring to my eyes when Dax and Mikhail pull me up on my knees and help me turn around on the mattress to face them. The explosion of sensation is simply too much as the toys move inside me, rubbing against each other and sending sparks of electricity into my overly sensitive folds.

I stare up at Nikolai, shaking my head as the oppressive feeling of the dildos expands and pounds through my abdomen, shooting bolts of lightning that make me spasm with a painful need for release.

Dax and Mikhail proceed to put leather mittens on my hands and strap them to the waist belt. All the while, I keep staring at Nikolai with tears streaming down my cheeks, my nostrils flaring as my breaths come in staggered drags.

He doesn't say a word, doesn't twitch a muscle. He's impassive and uncompromising until Dax and Mikhail step aside. Only then does he approach and sink to his haunches before me, grabbing my chin in a hard grip that matches his stern expression.

"You're mine. Mine to use, mine to hurt, and mine to torment. I'll take care of you too, but right now I want you to feel my power through and through. I'm your master, and you'll take whatever I give you, whenever I give it. Are we clear?"

I nod in his hand, sniffling as the tears run faster. But it's not because his words scare me; it's because I can't contain the emotions swelling inside me.

Mikhail breaks the trance. "Sure I can't get you another girl? I have great ones who have just finished their training, and I can give you a good price."

Nikolai watches me like he can see into the very depths of my soul as he answers Mikhail. "I only need this one." He picks something off the mattress, and then rough jute material dulls my senses as he pulls a small sack over my head and tightens it around my throat, fastening it with a knot.

"Put her in the box," he says, and Mikhail and Dax hoist me up by the arms and carry me across the room.

Whatever little light the sack offers fades as they lay me in the box, between four solid walls. I'm grateful to feel that the insides are padded, so my skin won't scrape against the rough wood as I jostle about in the crate. It reminds me of the trunk on the night they took me—the pillows Mikhail used to pad the confined space and the uncertainty. I know as little about where I'm going and what's going to happen to me as I did back then. But there's one big difference. This time, I'm not being taken away from Nikolai; I'm being brought to him, wherever that may be.

Nikolai's scent drifts past the jute as he leans down and pushes the fox under my arm—the same teddy he gave me when he sent me off to be kidnapped and trained for his pleasure.

Then he's gone, and the darkness becomes complete as the lid is placed on the box. Sharp sounds of nails and hammers fill the space as they seal it closed.

"See you soon, my sweet *Lisichka,*" Nikolai says just before the box lifts off the ground and I'm carried away.

EXTENDED EPILOGUE

Four months later

My breath is coming in ragged drags as I step into the presidential suite at the Four Seasons Hotel in Paris. Wiping the towel around my neck at my sweaty forehead, I halt in my tracks as I enter the living area and hear Nikolai's voice.

"I want you to go out and buy yourself the perfect dress for tonight."

Looking up, I find him leaning back in the upholstered chair behind the desk across the room. The vision of his effortless authority always takes me aback, speeding up my already racing heart even as it pulls me into a state of calm submission. But what has the biggest effect on me today are his words.

"But I've nev–" I stop myself. He already knows I've never gone out without him despite being allowed to do so for a month now.

"Usual procedure for going out alone," he adds, reminding me of the exact reason I've never gone out.

"I have plenty of pretty dresses in the wardrobe," I try.

"This is not about the dress, and you know it. I've given you a month to build up to this, and I'm done waiting."

Breathing a shuddery sigh, I nod and lower my gaze. "Yes, Master."

"Daniil will look after you." Nikolai gestures at the man who is standing quietly to the side with his hands folded before him. "He'll even help you with the transactions if you need it and speak on your behalf."

I cast a glance back at the brawny guard, who has quietly followed me to the downstairs gym, waited discreetly at the side while I did my third round of yoga this week, then followed me back up. He's always there, yet I've never spoken a word to him, and that's probably why I've never gone out—because of the thing I have to ask him to do in order to do so. Or maybe because of the humiliation that will follow.

"It's time you get used to it. I don't want you stuck inside the hotel all day when I'm away."

"Okay. I understand, Master," I say politely even as my blood swooshes with nervous energy.

"Good girl. Now come here and get your reward." He gets up and holds his hand out to me.

Gingerly, I pad across the room to stand in front of him.

Grabbing my waist, he lifts me to sit on the desk and leans down to kiss me. "Did you like the yoga instructor?" he asks as he breaks the kiss.

"She was great," I say, my lips tipping up in a shy smile as he curves his hand around my cheek and strokes his thumb along my skin.

"Good. We'll be staying here for another two weeks, and I'd like to keep you limber." As if to test the fruits of the many hours of private yoga lessons he's paid for, he sets my feet up on the wooden surface and slowly pushes my knees apart.

Folding my hands around his neck, I hold on as he spreads me wide open, and I vaguely notice a door closing behind us as Daniil takes the cue and leaves the room.

Slowly, he drags his fingers up my inner thigh to caress my pussy, eliciting a flurry of sparks and shudders under the thin fabric of my yoga shorts. Then he moves up, over my stomach and chest, wrapping his hand around my throat, squeezing as he slowly pushes me down to lie on the desk.

"Open your mouth, little slut," he orders, leaning down to hover his lips right above mine.

A staggered breath stutters in my constricted throat as I part my lips and lean my head back to grant him access. Heat and humiliation twine and twirl inside me as he spits in my mouth.

"Don't swallow," he demands, drawing his head back a little to watch the spit glide down my tongue. "Tonight, you're gonna wear the ring gag, and every man at the table is going to spit into your mouth before we start eating. Then, you'll sit there, patiently waiting with their spit stuck on your tongue, until we're done."

My heart speeds up to a frantic rhythm that makes my chest shake as I stare up at the dark promise in his bright blue eyes.

He spits again, and I pant hard at the dirty feeling of

his saliva trickling down my tongue. "What does a little slut say when she gets to taste her master's spit?"

"Thank you," I say in a slurred voice, still not swallowing since I haven't gotten permission.

"Good little *Lisichka*." Releasing my neck, he presses a finger under my chin and closes my mouth. "Swallow. And go get ready to hit town. I want you in the prettiest evening gown you can find tonight."

I swallow his spit and nod.

"And don't touch my cunt without permission." He rubs his hand against my pussy, drawing a moan from my throat.

"Of course, Master," I say in a breathy voice, confirming what has become second nature: obeying his command.

* * *

After a much-needed shower and lots of contemplation, I get dressed and go into the living room with my heart pounding in my chest. Nikolai is gone, as expected, but he's not the man I'm looking for. The man I need is standing close to a wall, eyes trained straight ahead, hands folded in front of him.

"I'd like to go out," I tell the towering man with arms the size of trunks hidden behind an expensive suit.

Not batting an eye, like this is yet another standard task of his job, Daniil picks up two items from the side table. "Which one would you like?"

I shift my eyes back and forth between the small tongue plate, which will render speech impossible, and the leather panties with two attachments. When I left the bathroom, I thought I had made my decision—there's no way I'm going dress shopping on my own without being able to speak. But as I glance up at the impassive man who is to insert the two dildos, I waver. I don't know why the idea makes me so uneasy. I've had plenty of men doing humiliating things to me, but I guess being back in the real world has restored some of my modesty.

"I don't know," I say, feeling lost.

He doesn't reply, just stands there, holding up the degrading items. I think five minutes pass as I stare back and forth between him, the tongue restrictor, and the crude panties. Looking at the items, I know which one I prefer—by far. But as I close my eyes and imagine having to navigate being outside on my own and communicating with people in a store—women who expect me to be independent and outspoken—I just can't do it. So I open my eyes and point to the panties. "That one." Then I hurry into the bedroom for no apparent reason other than not wanting to face the man about to dole out the humiliation I just asked for.

Of course, he follows me. Heavy steps thud against the floor as he enters the room.

I jump onto the bed and pull the covers over me, hiding like a child. I have no idea what's gotten into me. Nikolai has let other men touch me on several occasions. But it's always been light play—stroking my breasts and curves or playing with my clit—and he's always been there at my side, pulling the strings, demanding my submission. Even in the dungeon, when I learned to submit without protest, I only submitted openly to two men, and now I need to willingly subject myself to a man I have never even spoken a word to until now.

So I stay under the covers as he shoves up my skirt, finding me bottomless, my pussy already bare because I knew what was coming.

I whimper as he lifts my legs, one at a time, to put the leather panties on me. His hands are rough and calloused like Dax's, and I try to imagine that it's him as the leather is pulled up over my legs. But the illusion won't stick. Because Daniil's guttural Russian accent is nothing like Dax's American drawl.

"Lift your hips," Daniil says.

"I can't do this," I say, scooting farther under the covers and kicking my legs to free them of the leather panties.

"Do you want me to tell Nikolai that you've been a disobedient girl?"

Shit. I freeze. Because he's right. If I don't do this, I'll directly disobey Nikolai, and there's no way I can do that. So I slowly pull out from underneath the covers and face the man about to invade my body. I can't escape this, but there's one thing I can ask for to make it a bit easier.

"Will you please tie me up before you do it?" I ask in a barely audible voice. I remember the restraints of Dax's exam table—how they always calmed me. Maybe they will this time too.

A smile pulls at his impassive features, just for a quick moment before it's gone again. Then he leaves the room, and I scoot back down and turn around to lie on my stomach. I pull the covers over my head again, hoping not seeing will ease the humiliation. As I lie there waiting in the darkness of the covers, a twisted sort of anticipation stirs within me. Because as much as I hate this, I also want it. The humiliation and the helplessness at the hands of a stranger. Mikhail has trained me well. The need is deeply conditioned within me, and as I involuntarily clench my thighs, I realize I'm already wet.

Daniil returns a minute later, and I gasp as he pulls my right hand from beneath the covers and attaches a leather cuff to it. He makes quick work of attaching the cuff to the corner of the bed, where chains remain from when Nikolai spread me out in an X and spanked and fucked me last night. Then he does the same to the other and attaches leather cuffs to my ankles too. Before fastening my legs further, he pulls the panties back over my feet, and the appendages slap crudely against my legs as he moves the leather up around my thighs.

"No," I whimper in a protest that doesn't sound very convincing.

It doesn't stop Daniil. He proceeds to attach the ankle cuffs to a spreader bar instead of the corners of the bed, then hoists my waist up and bends my legs to make me lie on my knees with my ass in the air. Before I can try to stretch my legs again, he sits behind me, knees on the spreader bar, locking me into place.

I squirm against the restraints—an instinctive reaction—as he prods the first dildo against my pussy. Shame courses through me as he pushes the tip into my wet opening. But instead of dragging me into despair, the shame seems to coil around the intrusion, gathering more liquid heat at my core.

I feel him leaning over me and hear the slide of the

drawer in the nightstand opening. A moment later, his hand is on my ass, spreading my cheeks apart with one hand while dripping cold lube onto my narrow opening with the other. Tensing, I burrow further into the covers as if it would alleviate the devastating sense of defeat.

The helplessness is stark as he positions the smaller of the two dildos against my ass and presses. The tip pops straight in. Nikolai has kept up Mikhail's training well, and I only need a little preparation to take his massive cock. This dildo is nothing compared to his size. But the small size of the dildo does nothing to alleviate the terrible humiliation as Daniil applies pressure and pushes it in.

I whimper and strain my legs against the unforgiving spreader bar, but nothing gives, and my world becomes a narrow tunnel of obtrusive invasion, sparks of unwanted pleasure, and humiliation as he starts pushing at the other dildo too, sinking both deep inside me, filling me to the brim.

Once they're in, he doesn't do more to tease or test. He simply pulls the leather up over my butt and stomach and straps the buckles at my waist.

"All done," he says and starts releasing me from the restraints.

Once I'm free, I just lie there for several minutes, barely breathing, waiting for him to leave. When I don't hear receding steps and can't stand the waiting anymore, I slowly slip out from beneath the covers. Every tiny movement jostles the dildos inside me, making them rub against each other through the narrow wall separating them.

My face is burning hot, my pussy throbbing, as I sit up.

"Will you please leave," I say, keeping my eyes lowered as I scoot out to sit on the edge of the mattress with my back to him.

"I need to keep an eye on you," he simply says.

Gingerly, I stand up, supporting myself with a hand on the wall as I struggle to find my balance. I take a step and yelp at the bolt of sensation shooting through my stomach. One more, and I pause and close my eyes, breathing heavily through the intense feeling of the dildos moving.

Releasing the wall, I step farther into the room, toward the bathroom, and each step is a staggered movement. "I—I can't go out like this," I say in a weak voice, grabbing onto a chair.

Taking one more step, I nearly trip as the jostling sensation in my lower body makes my muscles jerk.

Daniil is at my side in an instant. "You won't fall on my watch," he reassures, placing a hand under my elbow.

I glance up at him and toward the walk-in closet a few steps away. The rest of the walk almost seems insurmountable, and so does getting into my remaining clothes. And I have no idea how I'm going to walk around the city like this.

Looking up at him again, I say, "Can I change my mind and get the tongue restrictor instead?"

"I'm sorry," he says, giving a regretful shake of his head.

My face falls. Training my eyes on the floor, I just stand there, feeling hopeless, until Daniil speaks again.

"Do you want me to help you get dressed?"

I give a slight nod, and for the next two hours, I give in to his steady support as he helps me get dressed and ready to leave, leads me to the car, and lets me lean on his arm as I go from store to store.

The tongue restrictor would have been better, indeed, because I can't seem to speak a word as my whole body pulses with aching need. Daniil ends up handling all the communication with the store people, letting me hide in the changing room while they rush around to find the right dress for me.

I'm tempted to pick the first dress that fits, but it's far from perfect, and even desperate as I am to go back to the hotel, I can't make myself disobey Nikolai like that. He wants the best. So I endure three trips to different stores before I can finally collapse in the backseat of the SUV with the right dress in a garment bag beside me.

When we get back to the hotel, my cheeks are flaming, and white-hot need is pounding and pulsing in my whole body. The dildos aren't enough to make me come, and I'm as grateful as I'm disappointed. Because coming without permission would be the greatest transgression of all. But the need pulsing through me makes me desperate for release, and as Daniil helps me lie down on the bed, I think I'll almost be able to come anyway just by squeezing my thighs together.

"Take them out, please hurry," I beg, all my modesty having gone out the window.

"They have to stay until Nikolai returns."

"No," I gasp with wide eyes. "I can't take it; it's too much. I'll come if they stay in."

"I'm sorry, but that's my order."

"Please," I beg, pressing my hands to my face as I squirm on the mattress. "I can't... I just... There's no way I can stop it."

"Do you want me to help you not to come?" he asks.

"Yes," I say through bated breaths.

Daniil once again attaches the leather cuffs to all four of my limbs along with a collar around my neck. This time, the wrist cuffs go on the collar with a small chain, and the ankle cuffs go onto the spreader bar again, so wide apart I can't rub my thighs together. Finally, he hands me the fox teddy, pulls the comforter over me, and tucks me in, telling me to let him know if I need anything.

The next hour, as I wait for Nikolai to return, is painful. I flit back and forth between somewhat calm moments and stretches of panicked despair. One minute, I lie frozen on the mattress, staring at the ceiling, afraid to stir the pulsing need that has just calmed somewhat. Then I accidentally move something, and the need bursts back alive, and I succumb to desperate tears as I writhe against the restraints, seeking release, trying not to seek it, and being unable to find any. When Nikolai finally returns, I'm so desperate I think I wouldn't be able to keep myself from coming if I were able to reach climax.

"Please, please, please," I beg, following him with my eyes as he moves through the room and rounds the bed. "Please make me come. I can't take it anymore. Please."

"Shh," he soothes, crawling under the comforter to lie beside me.

The tears break free anew as he strokes my cheek,

174

and I burrow my head against his chest as I weep, my hips grinding against the mattress as burning need flares at my core.

"Such a good girl. I'm so proud of you," he tells me, stroking my stomach. "Are you ready to go to dinner soon?"

"No. I can't. I—No!" The desperation inside me doubles as I consider going any longer like this. My every muscle is taut with the need to come, trembling from the strain of denial, and my skin is sleek with sweat. "I can't," I repeat. "Please don't make me."

"Shh." He presses a soft kiss to my temple before lifting his head and calling out, "Daniil."

The guard is in the doorway a few seconds later.

"Remove the panties," Nikolai tells him.

I lean out from Nikolai to aim my begging eyes at him. "Can't you do it? Please. I can't take any more. It's too much."

Nikolai strokes my hair out of my damp face. "You'll take more because I want you to," he tells me with confidence as if it's supposed to be a reassurance. "Daniil won't be the last man to touch you tonight, but I'll be at your side the whole time."

His words send me crashing into hollow sobs, shuddering and jerking against him as Daniil removes the ankle cuffs, then pulls out the dildos and removes the panties.

"Such a good girl," Nikolai soothes, stroking and rocking me all the while. "You want to please your Master, right?"

"Yes," I say, clutching his shirt as the urge to do just

that swells inside me. "I do."

"Good. The guests will arrive in an hour, and the makeup artist is already here." He gently helps me off the bed and tucks me into his side, supporting me as he leads me to the huge bathroom. "But first, we need to get you cleaned." He helps me into the large shower stall and detaches the cuffs from the collar to attach them to a ring in the ceiling that seems to be conveniently in place in every hotel we visit.

"Do you want me to help ease the discomfort?" he asks, flicking a finger through my dripping wet folds.

Knowing how he'll do it, I want to say no, but there's no way I can resist the caring tone in his voice. And I do need something to calm the pounding energy at my core. Badly. So I nod and speak in a tiny voice. "Yes please, Master."

He removes the collar and cuts off my clothes with a switchblade, then takes his time removing his own clothes in a more formal manner.

When he grabs the handheld shower and screws on the knob that controls the temperature, I close my eyes, bracing myself.

I scream the moment he screws the other knob and icy cold water hits me. He sprays the water all over my body, and I cry again as the cold bites deep into my bones. I writhe and jerk against the restraints, but it's no use. I'm stuck in place. Forced to take the icy spray.

"It's okay, I've got you," he soothes once he turns the temperature up and steps in with me, wrapping a supportive arm around my waist.

I sink into him, weeping like a child as he soaps us

both up, then takes his time rinsing with warm water.

"Did that help?" he asks as he unbuckles the wrist cuffs and helps me out of the stall.

Sniffling and biting my lower lip, I nod. The pounding heat between my legs has died down. I feel it lurking in the shadows, ready to come alive at the slightest touch, but the tingling sensation that remains is bearable.

"I'm glad to hear that." Taking my head between his hands, he kisses my forehead, then wraps a towel around me and calls out for Daniil to bring in the makeup artist.

* * *

Half an hour later, I'm all dressed up in my new gown, hair styled, and makeup brightening my face. Nikolai takes me by the hand and guides me to the set table in the dining room, where he helps me to my knees on a pillow.

"Open your mouth and stick out your tongue," he says, crouching in front of me.

He unscrews the top ring on the tongue piercing and attaches a small plate on some new toy I don't recognize. It's some kind of face harness, but there's no leather panel to cover my mouth as usual. I whimper as he pushes a large silicone-covered ring between my teeth. *A ring gag.* The feeling is obtrusive, and even more so as he fastens the straps around my head, locking my jaw in place around the ring. My mouth is stuck in a wide-open position, and with the small plate attachment depressing my tongue, I can barely swallow, let alone speak a single word.

"I really love this piercing," he says, stroking the sides of my mouth as he studies the ring gag. "It really makes you so much more helpless."

He's right. I feel the helplessness deep in my bones whenever he restricts my tongue. It's so subtle yet blaring to my senses, having movement that I've always taken for granted restricted. I never realized how much I moved my tongue until he used the muzzle on me the day he took me from the dungeon. It makes swallowing hard and speech all but impossible. Whenever he takes me out with the discreet tongue restrictor in my mouth, I go soft and pliant. No one can see the small plate surrounding my tongue, but I can feel it. It keeps me quiet at his side and tugs me deep into a heady trance of submission, constantly tethered to him and his command.

But this ring gag is new, and trepidation creeps along my spine as I consider the implications. I know he wasn't making idle threats when he said that his guests would be spitting in my mouth, and with my tongue trapped, there'll be no way for me to swallow until the spit slides to the very back of my throat.

"So pretty," Nikolai says. "But we'd better do something about this," he adds as he swipes a thumb along the side of my mouth to catch a bit of spit that's already dripping out.

He proceeds to strap a collar onto my neck, backward to position the ring at the back of my neck. Then he attaches a small chain to the back of the harness and to the collar ring, forcing my head slightly backward.

It makes it easier to swallow the saliva gathering at the back of my throat, but I'm not sure it will prevent the mess of me drooling fully.

Finally, he finishes off by attaching leather cuffs to my wrists and gathering them behind my back.

Stepping in front of me, he watches the result. "Perfect. Now, be a good girl and stay there while I go greet my guests."

He leaves the room, and a few minutes later, I hear voices drifting through the suite. I squirm on the pillow as steps close in, squeezing my eyes shut as I hear them enter the room.

"Open your eyes, my sweet *Lisichka*," Nikolai says, and the feeling of his warm hands cupping my cheeks as he steps behind me is a welcome relief. They provide some much-needed stability as I go against all my instincts and peel my eyes open to look up at a man I've never seen before.

His eyes roam over me with unrestrained hunger— my distended mouth, my pushed-up breasts, and my every curve. Being dressed is a small mercy, but even so, I feel stark naked as I try to clench my jaw around the ring gag and my mouth remains wide open.

"You may greet her," Nikolai tells the stranger, who leans down and hovers in front of my face, his hot, minty breath seeping into my mouth.

Pfft.

I yelp as he spits. Right onto my tongue. Jerking, I try to move my head—farther back, forward, to the side. Anything to rid my tongue of the sensation of a stranger's spit sliding down it. But Nikolai tightens his hands around my head, and the spit is stuck in my mouth. I can't even move my tongue to swallow it.

"Can you feel how helpless you are," Nikolai says in a low voice as he leans his head close to my ear. "You can't even swallow Luc's spit. All you can do is wait for it to slowly slide to the back of your mouth. Then maybe you can swallow some of it."

The wet sensation on my tongue intensifies as Nikolai draws my attention to the crude humiliation, and my breaths come in loud drags through my open mouth. But it's not just the need to flee that has me breathing hard. My breaths deepen as I sink further into that fluffy space where nothing but Nikolai's demand matters. And when the next man spits in my mouth, I wriggle on the pillow as a slow hum stirs at my core.

"Good girl," Nikolai croons, stroking his thumbs along my cheeks. My eyes glide shut as I sink into the fluffy space under his control. He hums, enjoying my surrender, and the world slips away for a minute as we stay there, caught in the potent power exchange. "Now open your eyes again and face the next man who's going to spit in your mouth."

My eyes are swimming as I peel them open, and I blink a few times before I can get a good sight of the man in front of me. My breath nearly stops when I see him.

"Such a dirty little girl." Mikhail sinks to his haunches and retrieves a handkerchief from his suit pocket. "Drooling out of your mouth." He lifts the soft fabric to my chin and wipes the moisture away. "You'd better make sure my spit remains in your mouth, *Koshechka*, or I'll have to punish you."

I give him the slightest nod as I stare up at him, trapped by his powerful authority that has effectively broken me into pieces and built me up to become the person I am today. A person I sometimes don't recognize, yet a person I wholeheartedly want to be. Shame and regret may swamp me at times when I face the world and remember all the things I lost in the process of getting here, but whenever Nikolai wraps a hand around my throat and spears his command into me with the sharp acuteness of his eyes, the world slips away, and nothing else matters. Only his command.

Mikhail roams his gaze over the gag and the spit caught on my tongue. "Now, I can't make you ask for this, but I can ask you to accept it." He grabs my chin in his hand and leans close. "Would you like me to spit in your mouth, *Koshechka*?"

A dizzy, sort of cloudy sensation settles over my brain, and I let out a small sound that's supposed to be a "mm" as I nod my head.

"I'd be most happy to."

Pfft.

Another glob of spit lands on my tongue, mixing with the others and slowly gliding toward the back of my mouth. Humiliation and dark desire twine and twirl inside me, and when Nikolai steps around me to spit in my mouth himself, my head is swimming and heat is humming in my body.

The men take their seats at the table, but the only ones I notice are Nikolai and Mikhail, who sit on each side of me. Their voices mix with the clanks and clinks of plates, cutlery, and glasses as they start eating. It becomes a gentle soundtrack at the back of my consciousness as I sink into a floaty headspace. The only words that register in my muddled brain are when Nikolai leans down to say, "Such a good girl," or Mikhail lifts my jaw and asks, "Can you still feel my spit on your tongue?" then swipes a drop of saliva off my chin as he adds, "You'd better hope this is not it."

I can't even respond, and when Nikolai asks if I want to eat too, I just blink my blurry eyes up at him, barely understanding the question.

"Shall we feed my pretty girl, gentlemen?" Nikolai asks, and then he and Mikhail are turning me around on the pillow as the other two men round the table to stand in front of me.

I vaguely notice Mikhail turning a chair around and placing a steel dog bowl on it.

"Are you hungry, *Lisichka*?" Nikolai asks as he once again stands behind me, wrapping his warm hands around my cheeks to hold my head in place.

The question is rhetorical. I don't get a chance to answer before one of the men steps in front of me, pants already open, and slides his swollen cock past the ring gag, straight into my mouth.

My head clears somewhat at the sudden intrusion sliding over my tongue, into the remaining spit. "Ahh, ah," I protest, jerking my head against Nikolai's hands, trying to draw back. But I'm stuck. He holds my head firmly in place as the man in front of me drags his cock in and out through the ring, invading my mouth with his quickly growing erection.

"Don't worry, he's not gonna come in your mouth,"

Nikolai soothes, but his words barely register as the man presses the thick head of his cock against the back of my throat.

"Keep relaxing your throat," Nikolai tells me.

All my attention goes to my neck, forcing myself to relax even as I want to jerk and try to expel the sudden intrusion.

"Ahh, ah," I protest again, but the cock keeps advancing, and I can't do anything but keep still as to not trigger my gag reflex as he sinks into my throat and snuffs out my breath.

Moisture pools at the corners of my eyes as he stays there, and my hands clench and unclench at my back as I struggle to fight off the lurking panic that hovers at the fringes of my mind. I've had Nikolai deep in my throat several times, but the psychological effect of having a complete stranger there is severe.

As my air grows scarce, I start jerking again. But my head remains stuck in the vise of Nikolai's hands, so I start moving my shoulders instead, and as the desperation grows, I writhe my whole body. My chest stutters with the need to breathe, and I'm just about to lose control over my gag reflex when the man pulls out.

I cry out, heave in air, cry again, and breathe hard. I barely notice the sloppy sound of a man jerking off and a few splattering sounds as he groans and comes. All I know is that he's not coming on me as the urgency of breathing still racks through my body and makes me fall forward as Nikolai releases my head. He catches me with an arm around my chest as he sinks to his haunches behind me and swipes my hair out of my face.

"Such a good girl. Look what you did," he croons. With a gentle hand on my cheek, he nudges my head to the side, and my eyes go positively wide as I watch the dog bowl on the chair and the splatters of cum inside it. "You're gonna make all four of us come, and then you'll get to eat too," Nikolai says softly.

I shake my head ardently, still panting from the loss of breath. "Aah, aa," I protest again, making garbled sounds. But I don't get to protest for long. Banding an arm tightly around my shoulders, Nikolai holds me in place as a new man shoves his already hard length into my mouth. There's nothing I can do to stop it. Nikolai wraps his other arm around my waist, pinning me in place, and I sink into him as the intruding cock snuffs out my protests and my very ability to think. All I can do as he fucks my mouth is focus on breathing when I can and keeping my throat relaxed.

Spittle drips from my mouth as the man picks up pace. He doesn't sink deep into my throat like the first, but the pace with which he shoves in and out has me reeling, gasping, and whimpering.

"Such a mess you're making," Mikhail scolds, swiping at the long string of spit dripping down my chin toward my chest. "Get your hands up and clean up the mess," he demands, mocking me like he did so many times in the dungeon when putting my hands in the mittens and ordering me to open my fists.

I jerk against the cuffs on my wrists, whimpering as I remain stuck—stuck in the cuffs, stuck in the vise of Nikolai's arms, and stuck under the onslaught of the constant pounding in my mouth. *I can't,* I try to say, but the words become a nonsensical string of sounds around the intrusion.

"If you don't obey, I'll use your spit to use your ass," Nikolai threatens, and I pull more frantically as I blink my eyes around my surroundings and catch a few glimpses of men watching me. The stranger fucking my mouth and Mikhail aiming a stern expression at me. I feel utterly pathetic and helpless as I keep drooling, utterly powerless to do a thing, and the frantic energy builds as I think about how these men will see my most intimate opening invaded in a moment too. But as much as the humiliation pulls me into despair, it also gathers deep in my belly and sends liquid heat to my pussy.

A moan escapes me as the man fucking my mouth pulls out, and then I watch in horror as he comes into the dog bowl.

Before I can recover, there's a ripping sound of fabric being cut as Nikolai procures his switchblade and cuts a hole in the back of my dress. Just big enough for him to access my ass.

Grabbing my chin, Mikhail demands my full attention. "In a moment, we'll all be able to see what a little ass *shlyukha* you are as Nikolai shoves a finger inside your ass and you can't stop moaning."

"Ooo," I whimper, trying to say *no*. But Mikhail knows me well. He's the one who has trained me to like the depraved humiliation of having something inside my ass. And when Nikolai slides two fingers across my jaw to pick up a long string of spit, then positions them at my rear opening, all the dormant need from earlier in the day flares alive with a vengeance.

Nikolai tuts. "I barely even need to touch you. The thought alone drives you wild. You really are a dirty little ass slut."

Mikhail opens his pants, letting his rock-hard length spring free right in front of my face. He pulls my head forward to unbuckle the chain at the back of the harness, allowing my head free movement. "Suck it," he demands, moving my head back in place. "I want to see what a well-trained little slut you are, doing the job yourself."

Blood rushes to my face as I stare at his hard length, then glance up at him. As much as I'm embarrassed by the whole scenario, I want him. My blood pumps with eagerness to taste his cock again and submit to this man who pulled out the most shameful sides of me and made me embrace them. Slowly, I lean forward, pushing my open mouth over his very long length.

"All the way inside your throat," he says.

I gasp as Nikolai starts massaging my rear entrance, sending sparks and swirls of heat through my sensitive nerves. But I keep going, nonetheless.

"Ah, yes," Mikhail groans as I lean in to take him to the back of my throat. "That's it. Show me how much you've missed my cock."

I jerk as Nikolai pushes two fingers inside my ass. The advance is slow and measured, just like my movement as I take Mikhail into my throat, snuffing out my own breath. Sensation bursts through my core, and all thoughts vanish in a cloudy haze as I disappear into floaty subspace, accepting the total loss of control as these two men command my body.

"You are not allowed to come," Nikolai says as my

garbled moans grow longer and louder, revealing the building tension inside me. "Not until I say so." He shoves his fingers deep inside, making me gasp around Mikhail's cock.

Sensation rushes through me, crackling with sparks and heat at my core like an electrical device about to short-circuit. Or explode. It takes everything I have to stop the orgasm from rolling. I go rigid, tensing every muscle to keep the sizzle of pleasure from advancing and expanding. But still, I keep bobbing my head back and forth, relishing Mikhail's rumbling groan as I take him deep into my mouth.

Grabbing a fistful of my hair, he draws my head back and aims his cock at the dog bowl on the chair. White rivulets of cum spill into the bowl, sending trails of trepidation and desire twining and twirling along my spine at a hazardous pace that threatens to send me over the edge. Nikolai keeps his fingers still inside me, and I'm more than grateful for it. If he moved the slightest right now, I wouldn't be able to control a thing. And he knows it too.

"Good girl," he whispers into my ear, sending a shuddery shiver down my neck as his breath tickles my sensitive skin. "I know how hard it is to hold back. But in a moment, you'll get to come. Once I'm inside you and you've eaten every last drop of your dinner."

Mikhail sinks to his haunches in front of me and starts removing the ring gag.

I whimper as I try to close my mouth once the ring is gone, and Mikhail gently massages my jaw to help me along. "Slowly," he urges. A mischievous spark lights up his eyes. "Unless you're in a hurry to get your dinner."

I don't even know how to respond. My head is so fuzzy I can't seem to discern whether I'm more disgusted or aroused by the idea of licking up the contents of that bowl. And when Mikhail places it in front of me and I stare down at the thick layer of cum, I still can't decide. All I can feel is the instinctive need to obey as Nikolai says close to my ear, "Eat."

He draws out his fingers, eliciting a long moan from me as I lean down. Without my hands to balance me against the floor and my muscles being all loose and weak, I all but fall into the wide bowl, my forehead straight into the sticky mess. With a whimper, I try to lift my head out, but Mikhail forces me to stay in the mess as he wraps long fingers around the back of my neck.

"Eat," he, too, demands.

I start licking, slowly, wincing with disgust as I lap up the salty stickiness. I push a bit back against Mikhail's hand to get a small reprieve from the musky scent filling my senses, but he keeps me in place, head stuck in the mess, and my tongue keeps working on autopilot. Obeying.

But I go absolutely rigid the moment Nikolai positions his cock at my ass and starts pushing.

"No," I gasp, my voice slurring as I move my lips in the cum-filled bowl. "I won't be able to stop the orgasm."

"Then you'd better eat in a hurry."

Fuck. I clench my jaw for a moment as a roll of nausea flips my belly at the thought of lapping up the cum any quicker.

"You want to be a good little slut and please your

master, right?" Nikolai breaks through the tight rim of muscle, sending bolts of pleasure through my body, making me jerk between the two men.

"Yes," I say breathily.

"Then eat. I want your orgasm, but you're not getting it before the bowl is clean."

I don't think. I just obey as a haze of panic infiltrates my blurry mind. Licking quickly against the steel, I lap up sticky strings of cum as I tense to block out the aching, unignorable sensation of Nikolai shoving his very long, wide length into my ass.

"Thank me for feeding you once you're finished," he orders in a raspy voice that tells me he's already close to the brink himself. But Nikolai's control is staggering, and I know he'll be able to hold back, keeping me on this maddening edge until I've obeyed and emptied the bowl.

He starts moving. Slowly. Dragging in and out along my tight walls. Stretching me impossibly. Sending bolts of aching pleasure through my sensitive tissues.

I lap quicker, angling my head to this and that side to get every last drop of cum.

"Thank you, Master. Thank you for feeding me," I say between staggered breaths, trembling with the need to come.

"Is she done?" Nikolai asks.

Mikhail lifts my head by the hair and takes in the sticky mess on my face. "Almost." Swiping two fingers across my forehead, he wipes off the cum and brings his fingers to my mouth.

Knowing what I need to do to put an end to this torturous misery of pounding, aching pleasure, I eagerly open my mouth and take his fingers deep inside.

"You may come," Nikolai says, grabbing onto my hips as he picks up speed.

I moan around Mikhail's fingers as I come apart. Licking and sucking at the sticky cum only seems to drive the pleasure higher. I convulse and spasm, moan and groan around his fingers, then suck and lap again as pleasure pulses and pounds through my body.

Nikolai growls behind me just as I'm about to come down from the ledge, and the swelling of his cock and hardening thrusts sends me straight back onto it.

Pulling me half up to sit, Mikhail lets me rest against his shoulder as he leans down to shove a hand under my dress and stroke my clit.

I scream as pleasure tears at my body with a force that threatens to rip me apart. I can't take it, yet I want more of it. The orgasm is painful as it rips through my body with staggering jerks and painful convulsions.

I'm almost relieved when Nikolai pulls out of me. But then another man sinks down behind me. A new cock prodding at my ass.

"No, no, no," I whimper, turning my head to look at Nikolai. He's at my side now, scooting in to take Mikhail's place.

With an arm around my waist and a hand cupping the back of my head, he holds me close. "Shh, you need to take them all."

"I—I can't," I say with despair.

"Yes, you can. For me."

"I—" My words fail me as the new man presses into me. He easily sinks inside, and I vaguely wonder how

190

he's hard again—if they've all taken Viagra or if they're just that horny. But the thought disappears as quickly as it came. All I can do as the stranger fucks me hard and quick is to press myself into Nikolai, taking his comfort as he's the only thing keeping me steady in this whirlwind of tormenting pleasure and titillating degradation.

Mikhail cuts the front of my dress to get better access to my swollen nub. He keeps rubbing, sending me over the edge two more times as the two strangers take my ass.

By the time Mikhail is the one to push inside me, I'm crying—weeping like a child into Nikolai's shoulder. Somewhere along the way, he freed my hands, and I'm clutching his shirt with a might that's aching in my fingers. I need to hold on. I need his strength to stabilize me through the chaos that has banished all thought and control and rendered me this mindless, horny, desperate beast.

"One more," Nikolai says, releasing my head to reach under me and stroke my painfully sensitive clit. "And then we're done."

I don't even try to protest. I just keep crying and moaning as they force me to take another orgasm.

The moment Mikhail pulls out, I collapse in a heap on the floor. I'm spent and aching all over. A sweaty, shaking mess.

Nikolai hoists me into his arms and carries me to the couch. At first, I barely feel or hear anything. I only vaguely register that the other men exit the room, leaving me alone with my master. I'm exhausted. Drained. To the bone. My tears keep trickling down my cheeks, and I'm shaking like I've been stuck in a blizzard for hours.

But as Nikolai strokes my hair, whispering soothing words of 'good girl' and 'my precious *Lisichka*,' I find that it's not despair gnawing deep in my bones. It's just exhaustion. And as I curl up against him, accepting his comfort, I find safety and contentment.

Because no matter how rough or cruel the things he does to me are, they're coming from him. And I want it all. The truest, deepest testaments to his possession.

A vague memory flickers through my mind. A girl at a bar, searching for something. Yearning, but not quite knowing what she needed. I knew I'd like to explore kinks, but never in a million years could I have imagined that this level of depravity was what I needed to fulfill me and make me whole. If Nikolai had suggested it—even after all that kinky exploration of that first week—I would have run. He was right; I couldn't have handled the full depth of his demands. And even if he had eased me into it, I don't think I could have fully come to accept it while reflecting myself against the backdrop of the normal world.

No, the only way I could truly embrace this side of me and the full depth of it was in that dark, lonely dungeon where I was forced to shed all my dignity and identity—become a clean slate to be built up anew. Those two months might have been hell for me, but as I snuggle up against Nikolai and let his strength envelop me as I reel through the intensity of the night, I know I would go through it all again to be his.

"Thank you—for sending me to that dungeon," I

whisper, feeling the last remnants of the old me wither away and set me free.

"Hmm," he hums. A deep, appreciative sound. "I knew you'd get there." He trails his fingers up along my jaw, to my temple, settling his warm hand over my cheek. "I knew it deep down from the very first moment I laid eyes on you." Slanting his head slightly, he leans in, hovering his lips a breath from mine. "I knew you were perfect. The only girl in the world that could satisfy my darkness *and* my need to protect." He connects our lips in a sweet, tender kiss that robs my world of thought and renders me totally and utterly *his*. "The only girl I'll ever need."

Dear reader

Thank you so much for reading! I hope you enjoyed the book! Please leave a review (a couple of lines is all it takes). It would be a great help!

The next book in the Enslaved Series is about Dax, who is gifted a natural submissive to train. Pre-order "Break Me" today and sign up for my newsletter to get direct updates and exclusive sneak peeks into my writing projects.

Ella

www.ellajacobs.com/newsletter

ALSO BY ELLA JACOBS
Excerpt from Delivered to the Devil

He gave me to the devil but wanted me for himself.
Budapest was supposed to be my haven—a refuge from
my oppressive past. But the beauty of the city can't cover
up the dirt. Now I'm knee-deep in the muck, at the mercy
of one of the city's most powerful and ruthless men.

The moment I lock eyes with Istvan Gabor, I feel the
first trickle of a crushing darkness about to descend upon
my life.

But the corrupt politician is not the one who
awakens the dirty, depraved desires that put my life at
risk. It's the man who comes at night to prepare me for
Gabor's cruel games—a mighty, beautiful warrior named
Janos. He makes my worst nightmares come true even as
he breathes life into my soul and awakens the strongest
desires I've ever known.

* * *

A sound from within the apartment has ice-cold fear
slithering down my spine, stiffening my muscles and
snuffing out my sobs.

Footsteps approach.

I shoot up from the floor, so fast my vision darkens,
but I don't let it stop me. I shove my hand inside my bag

and grab the pepper spray just in time to see a massive, suit-clad man appear at the door.

For a second, I'm paralyzed, just staring at him—his steely gray eyes. They stare back, uncaring and cold. The same eyes that watched me through the darkness as my worst nightmare unfolded. They're even more striking beneath the light, and the angular lines of his face make his gaze seem even more severe. Sharp like a razor's blade and just as dangerous.

My heart pounds with a force that makes black spots dance in my vision as I take in his size. There's nothing nice or civilized about this man. He's pure, raw male strength. Not even his stately attire can hide it. There are no bulges or bumps like on the steroid-pumped guards manning the doors of clubs and bars at night. His arms are just massive. Everything about him is, yet somehow, his suit easily encompasses it all, making him seem almost elegant.

I blink to free myself from the trance, and instinct kicks in. Aiming the can at his head, I squeeze.

But I'm too slow. Or he's too fast.

Diving down, he tackles me. A low groan escapes me as he slams me into the drawer, my back connecting with hard wood. Before I can recover, I'm off the floor, the air knocked from my lungs as he throws me over his shoulder.

I bang my fists against his back, but it's like hitting a steel wall, hurting me more than him. My throat constricts, and tears glaze my eyes. I can barely see or breathe when he throws me onto the bed.

In a matter of seconds, he has me on my stomach,

pinning me in place as he straddles my ass and gathers my arms behind my back. All I can do is kick my legs behind me as my panting breaths grow more frantic, making me drag in more hair than air as powerlessness becomes a vise around my chest.

Locking my wrists together with one hand, he brushes the hair out of my face with the other. His touch is strangely gentle, but what's even more shocking is when he places his large palm on my cheek. No force, no pressing. It just lies there, warm and calm, as if he's trying to soothe me.

I realize my legs have gone still, and my breathing is working in slow, deep drags. It's wrong. *So wrong.* I want to soak up the tenderness, use it to level my shaken system, but I know it's a lie. There's nothing tender about this man. It's all a ruse to make me comply. I try to resist for a while, but as time ticks by, loud and long, my struggle fades. I simply can't hold it up. Finally, I sag beneath him and accept defeat—accept his comfort. Giving in is a relief to my straining muscles, but the consequence is a deep cut to my soul.

Quiet tears spill from my eyes as we once again wait, stuck in a warped kind of intimacy that rattles me as much as it soothes me. Silence descends upon the room, and the ticking of the clock becomes an eerie omen in the dead of night.

I don't realize another man is here until I hear him clear his throat from across the room. A whimper slips past my lips as I remember the scrawny man who was here the first night, and my muscles coil tight at the thought of his brutality.

The man on top of me swipes his thumb across my cheek. It's a small movement, but potent, nonetheless. It pulls my focus away from the threat of another man and back to him. Closing my eyes to this nightmare, I inhale deeply and release the built-up strain on an exhale as I let his heat seep into me.

But peace never lasts in nightmares. The sound of the front door breaks the silence, and firm steps announce that the waiting is over as a third man enters my nightmare.

The hand on my cheek disappears. Panic rises in its wake, and I realize the calm touch was the only thing keeping me steady. Now, cold dread slithers around my lungs, and I yelp as a new hand touches my face. But it's even more gentle than the first, fingertips caressing with feather-light softness, and my panic recedes like a wave pulling off the shore—not gone, but not quite there.

There's no mistaking the touch. It's the same fingers that explored my body a week ago. They are uncharacteristically soft for a man's hand. Maybe even manicured, I think as the back of the hand slides down my wet cheek. Their owner must be rich and vain—a control freak of the worst kind.

My gut twists at the thought, and a nauseous sensation rises at the back of my throat when the new man speaks. I don't understand his rapid Hungarian, but the voice alone says everything. Like the fingers, it is too refined—too calm for this chilling scenario. It resonates through the room with a steady kind of authority, commanding every particle without the slightest sign of brutality, eliciting a sort of power as rare as a white tiger.

Once again, I'm horrified to realize that dread is not my only reaction. Deep within the twisty sensation in my gut hides a slow hum that draws me toward the danger.

The Hungarian words must have been an order because they prompt the man on top of me to push up on his knees and flip me around. I'm irrationally grateful when he takes care to move my arms first, so he won't twist them in the process. I'm not sure if it's the gratefulness or if I'm still stuck in a trance, but I don't fight him. I remain limp, letting him place me in the new position and settle on top of me, carefully adjusting his weight so he won't crush me.

My hair is back in my face, sticking to my moist cheeks. This time, it's the new man who swipes a finger across my forehead to push it aside. He strokes several times to get all the hair away, and the slow movements lull me into a fleeting sense of safety, but when I open my eyes and stare into a pair of brown eyes glimmering with deceptive warmth, that feeling crashes.

My breath catches in my throat, and my heart slams into a violent rhythm.

I shouldn't be surprised. The first time I saw Istvan Gabor, I knew something was off, and when I found the note on the table, I knew he was the third man. I just couldn't come to terms with it.

Pressing his index finger to my lower lip, he coaxes me to release the air I'm holding in, and I let out a long, ragged exhale as I stare helplessly up at him.

He traces the same finger across my face, admiring the forms and contours.

"I've been looking forward to seeing you again," he

says in a whisper, as if the words are meant for my ears alone. Without taking his eyes off me, he waves off the man on top of me.

Not daring to move a finger, I lie completely still while Gabor roams his gaze up and down my body. His eyes are so sharp they seem to penetrate the layers of my clothes to caress my every curve and contour.

He issues another command, and the scrawny man approaches while the massive one moves to grab me under the arms and pull me into a sitting position between his legs.

Gabor takes a step back to enjoy the show as large hands grab my jacket. I let the massive man take it off as I stare into the dangerous depths of Gabor's eyes. A predatory glimmer flickers in the strange blend of warmth and cold, and the conflicting nuances seem to coexist quite naturally.

I swat at the arms a few times when they unbutton the collar on my waitress shirt, but it's not until the buttons over my breast pop open that I snap out of the trance. Suddenly, my eyes are no longer on Gabor. They're *everywhere* as I push and shove at the massive arms. But it's useless. With a thick arm around my waist, the man yanks me back into a rigid wall of muscle, pinning my arms at my sides.

Something rips, and I see buttons flying over my bed. I lock my arms around my waist to keep the shirt in place, but he simply pulls them away, and the fabric is gone within seconds. When the scrawny man grabs my shoes, I flail my legs so hard I pant with the effort. Again, it's pointless. I barely get a good kick in before I've lost both my shoes and pants.

Then goes my T-shirt. My panties. My bra.

I stare down, tears pooling in my eyes as I watch my naked body. The man behind me releases me, rustling with his own clothes, and I just sit there, staring at my nakedness in shock as I hug myself. When he grabs me again, his jacket is gone, sleeves rolled up to reveal olive-toned skin covered in black tattoos. I only catch a glimpse of the ink before I slap my hands to my face. For some reason, it's more important to hide my distraught expression.

The lanky man steps away as Gabor climbs up between my legs. Everything inside me coils tight as two fingers slide in between my folds. His touch seems to crackle with brutality, and I know he's not going to be gentle tonight even before he shoves straight in. A shriek tears through my throat and dies in a massive hand as the man behind me predicts my reaction. My head falls back onto his shoulder as he slams his hand onto my mouth, and I go absolutely frantic. I push and pull at his arms, and when nothing happens, I dig my nails in until I can't stand the feeling of breaking skin anymore.

Gabor drags his fingers in and out, slowly but forcefully, scratching at my dry walls. When a bit of moisture gathers down there, he adds a third digit and picks up speed. I buck my hips against the painful intrusion, but he pins me with a hand on my mound.

I scream, over and over into the massive palm. Slapping at the hands violating my body, I pull at the hand over my mouth, then shove at the one around my waist, but nothing works. My arms may be free, but they're useless. The realization is as devastating as the initial assault, and I wish they would have tied my arms. At least then I could cling to the illusion that I'm strong enough to put up a meaningful fight if I just got the chance.

Gabor is merciless. He keeps ramming his fingers in and out, and when one hand tires, he just uses the other. My only consolation is that my inner walls grow more wet as he goes. I try to convince myself that the moisture is a defense mechanism, but when Gabor rubs his thumb around my clit, my nether region sparks to life. I squeeze my eyes shut and try to force my focus away from my pussy, but sensations keep exploding in my nerve endings, and I become so wet there's a constant slippery sound coming from between my legs.

"You like this, huh?" Gabor mocks.

My eyes land on his, and the triumph I find there extinguishes the last remnants of my fight. I slump in the arms holding me, becoming as useless and weak as I feel.

My screams morph into quiet sobs, and the man behind me releases my mouth to curve his hand around my cheek. He touches me with the gentleness of a man comforting his lover. But that's not what's happening here. I know it, yet I can't resist the illusion. I desperately need it. So I turn to my side and bury my face against the warm shoulder, not caring who it belongs to.

My inner muscles start to contract, and a sob wrenches from my throat as I realize my body is about to betray me. I'm so exhausted I can't control it, and with a couple of sharp spasms, the orgasm rolls through me, turning my whimpers into a sick mix of despair and lust.

I can't take it—the violation, the betrayal, the shame. It all swirls in a nauseating whirlwind in my mind. I don't want my body anymore. It's vile and wrong—no longer mine—yet all I want to do is disappear into it. It's the only way to escape the scornful taunt of my mind. So that's exactly what I do. For a while, I let the feelings in my body consume me and allow myself to feel utterly shattered. I'm so broken I cling to the man behind me as I weep into his shoulder.

I vaguely notice Gabor pull his fingers out and get off the mattress. "Clean her up and get her to bed," he orders as the clicking of his shoes announces his departure. The slam of the door becomes the last sound I hear before my world sinks into numb stillness.

ABOUT ELLA

Ella Jacobs writes dark and kinky romance. Her books all center around Dom/sub dynamics, ranging from BDSM relationships with light dub con to pitch-black captor/captive stories with Stockholm syndrome and heavy non con.

What all her stories have in common is the emotional depth that makes them feel very raw and real. They will pull at all your heartstrings, maybe gut you and shock you, and take you through the emotional wringer.

Ella lives in Northern Europe, where she has been part of the BDSM community for many years. She lives her own age-gap romance with a stern, loving Dominant, who is always ready for some character analysis and rarely gets jealous when she falls in love with her fictional men.

Besides writing, Ella loves to play music and travel.

You can read more about her own experiences with the BDSM lifestyle on her website.

www.ellajacobs.com

ALSO BY ELLA JACOBS

Enslaved Series
Take Me
Break Me, *coming January 2025*
Heal Me, *coming Spring 2025*

Delivered to the Devil
Raw & emotional, heavy non-con

His in the Darkness
FREE dark and spicy novella

In His Cage
Dark abduction romance

Not Yours Trilogy
Raw & emotional BDSM romance
Not Yours to Keep
If I Were Yours

Made in United States
North Haven, CT
09 March 2025

66630318R00131